CU00652133

Published in Great Britain by
L.R. Price Publications Ltd, 2023
27 Old Gloucester Street,
London, WC1N 3AX
www.lrprice.co.uk

Cover artwork by L.R. Price Publications Ltd

Book by Stacey Jackson with Ruth Elkins.

ISBN-13: 978-1-916613-99-7

Dedication

Dedicated to my love and soul mate Henry, and my beautiful children Reid, Tyler, Liam and Caylie, my mom (the "authentic" Bubby) and brother Jonny, who have all been my rock and my greatest support.

HOW A GANGSTA RAPPER MADE ME A BETTER MOM

BY
STACEY JACKSON

with
RUTH ELKINS

THREE YEARS EARLIER...

The phone call came at 1:16 a.m. G.M.T.; 5:16 p.m. California time.

"Mrs. Bloom?"

I didn't recognize the voice. An American accent, about which there was nothing unusual or surprising. We are a North American family living in London; we have a pretty international life. But this woman's tone was serious.

I was exhausted, having been awakened from a deep sleep.

"Yes?" I said, barely awake and immediately assuming it was a random telemarketing call from American Express or something. "Who is this?"

"Mrs. Stephanie Bloom? Wife of K.C. Bloom?" Her inflection was official. Bad.

"Yes." I sat up quickly, as if a lightning bolt had struck me on the backside. I pulled the duvet around me, reached over to the nightstand and turned on the lamp. I immediately felt ice cold. I knew something was wrong – horribly wrong.

"Ma'am, this is Lieutenant Helen Shore of the L.A.P.D."

"L.A.P.D.? What's going on? It's late here."

"I know, ma'am. I am terribly sorry." I heard her take a long, deep breath. "Your husband was in a helicopter accident this afternoon. I am so, so sorry to tell you, Mrs. Bloom, that your husband died in the crash."

Chapter 1

"Let Me Show You Who I Am"

THREE YEARS LATER…

FRIDAY NIGHT. SOHO, LONDON.

WhatsApp from:

"Emily Bloom:

"X3+2x2−x(x2+2x−1) ???"

"Oh. My. Fucking. God!"

Tyson, one of my dancers tonight, stops by my dressing room at the same time as the *"Mom,-Help-Me-Now"* WhatsApp from my daughter pings on my phone. "How much do I love these?!" He strokes the hotpants hanging up with the rest of my costume. Gold. Sparkly. Perfect for tonight. And, I have to tell you, a serious bargain, too; I found them last week, for like two quid, on the sale rail at Primark.

"Oh, thank you, honey!" I say, not looking up from the phone.

"Don't know about equations," I type, frantically. Why does this kind of thing always happen when I'm trying to work?

"So, you don't think they're too much?" I say, looking up at

Tyson.

"Too much?!" Tyson holds up his hands, his perfectly manicured fingers splayed. "OH. MY. FUCKING. GOD!" He rolls his head dramatically. "Star Roberts, you should know by now that at The Pink Coconut *NOTHING* is *EVER* too much!"

I love my regular "Happy Hour" gigs at The Pink Coconut, Soho's best L.G.B.T. club. Usually, personal appearances like this are good because they're early, and early means I can go for dinner afterwards, or spend time with the kids. But, tonight, my daughter's math homework is slowing down my ability to get on stage. And I do need to get onto the stage, because the sooner I'm ON the stage, the sooner I can get OFF the stage and get into the car, to go to the Christina Wachman party.

Then WhatsApp pings again.

From:

Emily Bloom:

"Mom!!! I can't do my math! And I have to do my homework NOW. Kelly has already Snapchatted that she's done hers (emojis of crying faces x4). *MOM, YOU HAVE TO HELP ME!"*

Oy vey! Kelly Wachman again?

WhatsApp pings again.

"PLEEEEEASSSEEE, MOM... (emojis of hearts x10)*"*

And another:

"Pretty pleeeease! I (emoji of heart) *you sooooo much!"*

And another:

"Mom, I know you're in the club now, but PLEASE can you help me? And PLEASE tell me you're not wearing the sequin hotpants AGAIN? #Cringe."

Oy *vey! Stop pinging me!* Who, for the love of God, might know about long-division equations around here? Tyson? Nope, not even going to ask; Tyson is still mewing over my hotpants and checking himself out in the mirror.

"Red lipstick tonight?" Beaver, my make-up artist (yes, his name really is Beaver), waves a scarlet tube in my face. He makes a pouty face. "Matches the jacket…"

"I dunno," I say, "red is kinda harsh. I think red makes me look old."

"I promise it will NOT make you look old."

"Okay, we'll do the red," I say reluctantly, and think about all those red lipstick splotches my mom would leave on my kids' cheeks, as I tilt my face so that he can apply the stain.

"Er, Beavey, do you know anything about…" I look down at Emily's text message, "…er, polynomials?"

Beaver, who used to do make-up for Soho's drag queens, but now does ALL the faces of the rich and famous, doesn't skip a beat: "Oh, yeah, *love* their sound! *Am-az-ing!* Their look is stunning, too." He pauses and places his forefinger to the side of his mouth, momentarily in thought. "Do you know, I think my friend Martin is their stylist."

Oy vey is meir.

"On in five, Star." Roberto, the Pink Coconut stage manager, pops his head around the door, splaying his five fingers to underline exactly how many minutes I've got to get changed, miked up, out onto the stage and singing.

"Yep, sure," I say, before adding: "how's the crowd tonight, Roberto?"

Roberto purses his lips. "Darling, you know you've made it when you've got trannies dressing up like you." He blows me a kiss and disappears, his face immediately replaced by Tony's.

Tony Gironi is my long-term manager, and usually only turns up at my gigs when there's something big brewing.

"Hey, Tony, what's up?" I say, as nonchalantly as possible.

"Hey, Stephi-Star!" He always calls me that. Tony's a bit nuts, to be honest, and sounds like he's half asleep most of the time – but that's just his schtick, you know? He is a North Londoner, via his hometown of Miami, Florida, and has got that Woodstock *laissez-faire* vibe about him. I guess you'd say he was a bit of a hippy. Handsome, he looks kinda Grecian or Latino, with mid-length, wavy hair, olive-skin, jeans a bit too tight and shirts a bit too bright. He does yoga and meditates, and is always going on about clean living and chakras and shit like that, but usually only when he's totally off his face on Chardonnay and trying to chat up a girl half his age. He's not the most go-getting of managers, but I do love him, and have done ever since he took me on, when my first record made it onto the commercial dance charts.

"Yeah, just thought I'd drop by tonight, see how it's going..." he says, mysteriously.

"That's great! Great!" *Is there a point?*

"Just remember, ya never know who's watching..." He winks at me and then he's gone again.

Yep, he's right: give it as much energy as possible. Tony and I have long been discussing the next step for me: breaking into the mainstream. I jump up, grab the hotpants off the rail and pull them on, as quickly as possible, so I can get back to Googling *"long division for ten-year-olds"*.

Two minutes later and I'm not thinking about my stage energy; the only thoughts going through my head are, *Whoa, these things are frickin' IMPOSSIBLE*, and, *Why do they make things so hard for kids these days?*

Now my phone starts to ring. Next time I'm leaving the dumb thing in the car!

"Hi, Mom," says a deep voice, from the other side of the Atlantic.

"About to go on stage, Zack," I tell my nineteen-year-old son, who is at school in New York. "Can it wait?"

"Not really, Mom."

"Okay, what's the matter?"

"Er... Mom, are you wearing hotpants again?"

"Zack! Really? That cannot be why you rang me just before my set? What's the matter? Spit it out, honey."

"Uh, so, I'm in a bar and my bank card has been rejected," my son says. "The message on the screen said: *'insufficient funds'.*"

"Use your credit card," I say, pinching the phone between my ear and my shoulder, jumping up and down to try manoeuvring my feet into the six-inch platform heels.

"You froze my credit card this month, remember? You said I was spending too much. Thing is, Mom, do you even understand how much prices have gone up? I went to C.V.S., to buy a single tube of toothpaste, and it cost me seven bucks! Seven bucks, for toothpaste! It's not like it was in the old days, when you were in college."

Old days? Jeez!

"Plus, tonight is this semester's frat dinner and I literally have NO money, and I don't want to look like a putz. Anyway, Mom, seriously, you gotta help. Oh, and are you wearing those sparkly hotpants again?"

"Honey, get someone else to spot you some cash for tonight. I'll call you back."

For Chrissake, I can bloody well pull off wearing hotpants!

Another WhatsApp pings onto the screen, from:

"Emily:

"MOM? ARE YOU GOING TO HELP ME (emojis of

crying faces and love hearts and death skulls x10)?"

Roberto is back around the door, splaying three fingers and mouthing the word "THREE" at me, in case I'm not able to count. I grab the wireless mic receiver box and clip it to the back of my hotpants.

Ping!

WhatsApp from:

"Logan Bloom:

"Mom, Emily says you're wearing those hotpants again. Please tell me she's wrong."

Ping!

WhatsApp from:

"Zack Bloom:

"You literally can't leave me stranded in New York with no money (emoji of crying face)!"

Ugh! I throw the phone down on the dressing-room sofa and smooth down the sequins on the seriously small shorts. Beaver leans in and rubs some more bronzer into my thighs.

"You can NEVER have enough bronzer, darling," he laughs, smearing the dark-brown cream like Nutella on a bagel.

My phone rings again.

No. No. No. I'm not picking it up. I'm ignoring this call. Oh, God, my mother now, too? She usually doesn't even say hello.

"Darling, Gerald and I are packing for the cruise, and I just wondered what you'd suggest I wear for the Captain's Table

Dinner," begins the voice at the other end.

I knew this was going to happen. I knew it the moment I booked her that flipping cruise for her seventieth birthday.

"Mom, I am so sorry, but I'm about to go on stage!"

"Oh, well, dear, I do hope you aren't showing too much cleavage tonight."

Oh, my god! Not her, too?! "No, Mom," I say, "my jacket is firmly done up!"

Until the dancers rip it off, of course, before the first chorus of "Bombshell"! But then my boobs are completely covered in glitter and strategically placed rhinestones. It's called "disco tits" – totally on-trend. But I'm not going to get into that right now, especially not with my mother.

Roberto is back, head around the door, stressed expression, waving two fingers at me.

"Mom, I gotta go."

I hang up on my mother and type three messages on WhatsApp.

First to:

"Zack Bloom:

"Will transfer money in the next half an hour if you solve the following equation:

$X3+2x2-x(x2+2x-1)$*???* (emoji of winking face)

xoxo, Mom."

And then to:

"Emily Bloom:

"Your brother Zack is going to help you.

xoxo, Mom."

And finally, to:

"Logan:

"Yes, honey, I AM wearing the hotpants.

Love you. Bye. x."

Ha! Sorted.

I can hear the crowd in the club starting to cheer as the intro to "Bombshell" starts up. I throw the phone back onto the couch, run out of the dressing room, down the narrow corridor and out onto the stage.

TWO HOURS LATER...

"Stephanie!"

Christina Wachman glides across the grand entrance hall of her exquisite Chelsea home and embraces me tightly.

"So lovely we can hug again, isn't it? Thank you SO much for coming. *Mwah! Mwah!*" She kisses each cheek loudly, before standing back and giving me the once-over. "Well, you look amazing tonight; very... er... sparkly."

I glance down at my chest, and see that the remnants of the "disco tit" look are hanging on, like hard-to-remove limescale on the inside of a kettle. *Don't let her get to you,* I hear my late husband's voice say in my head.

Thanks, sweetie, I reply, silently.

I still hate going to these things on my own.

Christina and Gregory Wachman's house, off Drayton Gardens, is decked out to the nines and the place is buzzing. A large, oval table in the centre of the hallway overflows with exquisite floral arrangements and tall, flickering candles.

Black-jacketed waiters scuttle around with trays of champagne and cocktails, offering delicious-looking canapés of Wagyu beef burrito and exquisite burrata, topped with tiny, edible flowers, to immaculately dressed guests. We serve a similar burrata dish with flowers at our restaurants.

We have two restaurants, actually: one in London and one in New York; both are called Café Michael. They are a modern twist on the great American steakhouse, but the London one also has a kind of Viennese *Fin de Siècle* vibe about it, while the New York one is more "Great Gatsby" glam. They are the places to see and be seen in both cities, and they were my husband's pride and joy. Anyway, the burrata thing with the edible flowers always goes down well with the Chelsea crowd, like the Wachmans.

Christina snaps her fingers at a girl who steps forward and takes my coat. "Lovely to see you, darling," she says again, turning toward the door and the next guest in line.

I stand there in the middle of the room for a moment, trying to brush off the remnants of my sparkles, which are dangling like glittery, hanging chads. Damn, I thought I'd eradicated the Club Singer look and effortlessly transitioned into Chic Chelsea Mum on the way over. Obviously not.

"Steph!" I hear a voice coming in my direction and look up. It's Alejandro; he's waving vigorously.

Alejandro Costardo is one of my best friends. He's married to Timothy Green, a Mayfair hedge-funder who FINALLY came out a few years back, although frankly we'd all known he was gay for years. Their daughter Constanza (surrogate, not adopted) goes to school with Emily. Alejandro has an interior design consultancy. He's super-fabulous and, frankly, hot as—

"Oh, thank God you're here!" He leans in, smelling fabulous as usual, and sighs in my ear: "Tim's working again, of course. What are you doing? Stop scratching yourself to death," he says, brushing my hand away from my chest; "no one likes a rash, dear."

I giggle and give him a hug. Christina's right: post-Covid we will *never* take hugging for granted again. "So, who else is here?" I ask, scanning the room for friendly faces.

Alejandro always likes to arrive early at parties, for maximum gossip-gathering. He folds his arms. "Well, darling, let's see... We've got the hedgies, bankers and lawyer crowd, their wives... none of their mistresses... Of course, our esteemed hostess is also here." Alejandro nods in the direction of Christina Wachman, hugging more guests by the door.

"The house manager was telling me she's now got an entire floor dedicated to her walk-in wardrobe! Can you believe it?!" Christina is well known in Chelsea circles for never wearing the same designer dress twice, and she wouldn't be seen dead in Zara which, frankly, is her loss, in my opinion.

Alejandro spins me around to look in the other direction. "We also have Lauren Henderson, who is looking particularly fabulous *ce soir* in a black jumpsuit – Dior, I should say. Although, let's face it, she's probably boring EVERYONE about her glory years in New York."

Lauren is on the school P.T.A., like Christina and I, and was once a highly ambitious corporate lawyer in the U.S. But she never made it past the associate level before moving to London. She is now the mother of three boisterous teenage boys, and her own frustrated career ambitions have been re-channelled into her offspring.

Alejandro spins around again, and gestures in the direction of a woman in a hot-pink gown. "A-ha! And let us not forget the great Amanda May!" he says. "An almost perfect specimen of the High-Spending Helicopter Mom, with a brood of absolutely perfect children: Felicity, the eldest, who got into Yale last year, and the AMAZING Myla, whose eleventh birthday party will only be remembered for Myla performing the entire *Frozen* back-catalogue, and the rumours afterwards that she was going to be on *The Voice, Kids.*"

I laugh at his sheer, unflinching portrayal of the people circulating throughout the room. "Alejandro, you're so bad," I whisper, "but I do love you."

"Well, darling, we're not exactly in their league, now, are we?" he says. "But I do like getting invited to their parties."

Alejandro's right: we're not in the Wachmans' league, but we still live very nice lives. I have a great house in Chelsea. Okay, there's no basement pool, but it's big enough and really "haimish". My kids go to private school. And, when my husband died, between the profits made by the two restaurants plus a small life-insurance policy, I was able to keep on some "support" staff: Jan, the driver (who makes me believe that I can be in three places at one time, plus is absolutely necessary because I seriously haven't figured out this driving-on-the-wrong-side-of-the-road thing, despite all my years living over here); Candice, my husband's long-time personal assistant; and Beverly, our incredible nanny/housekeeper. Without them and my mother, I don't think I could have survived my husband's death... or continue with anything, really.

"Stephanie! Alejandro!" says a voice behind us. Giovanna! Lovely, lovely Giovanna. Thank goodness for Giovanna, my other best friend in London. An Italian princess who couldn't give a crap about the competitive hedgie wives, because she's...

well, she's royalty and she's above all that — you know, even if the Italians *technically* don't have a royal family anymore.

Giovanna — in pale-peach, silk Alexander McQueen — embraces me, before reaching over to a passing waiter for a glass of champagne. She hands it to me. "My dearest Stephanie! You cannot be without champagne on an evening like this!" She gives me a wink.

Gio and her husband Pietro are my support crew at parties like these. Sticking with them prevents me looking like a Black Widow, poised to ensnare any number of wealthy, married men into my dastardly, widowy web. As if...

And, you see, I never really felt like I was ever one of the traditional Chelsea "Sloanies", spending their days schpatzing up and down Chelsea's fashionable Sloane Street. We own the place in the neighbourhood where they all go to eat, and running a successful restaurant is tough. So, while our kids go to the same schools, and we get invited to the parties they host (and, don't get me wrong, I am also no stranger to Sloane Street... and I do love a bit of shopping), I've always felt a little bit on the periphery.

You can imagine the mixed reactions when, at the age of forty, I finally embarked on my dream of releasing a record. It was something I always wanted to do, from the time I started writing songs by ear, at twelve years old, on the stand-up piano my grandmother bought me for my birthday. The intention was for all the profits to go to a kids' music charity, and it did. But then something odd happened: one of the singles on my album somehow got remixed by a couple of dance music D.J.s affiliated with the charity, and suddenly I was sitting between Lady Gaga and the Scissor Sisters on the dance-music charts! Gigs and festival tours started to flood in, and I got calls from major-league producers, to write and record original music. I couldn't believe what was happening: I was becoming a "pop star" in my forties.

I can feel my phone vibrating in my clutch. I open it and take a sneaky peek at the screen.

"*Franz.*" The restaurant's financial director, Franz. *Really? At this hour?* Franz is still a BIG fan of the fax.

I thought it might be Tony, calling me back; I spoke to him in the car, on the way over here. To be honest, it sounds like he has some pretty cool stuff on the boil for me: a few bigger gigs up north, a photoshoot for a music mag and a couple of podcast interviews. Everything is pointing in the right direction.

Anyway, it isn't Tony, it's Franz. And Franz can wait. I slip the phone back into my bag.

Christina Wachman's husband Greg saunters over. "Hey, Steph." He leans in a little too close and kisses me on the cheek, looking straight at my chest. "Been… singing… tonight?" he says, as if I were a child who just performed solo in a high-school musical. I nod, internally rolling my eyes. It always seemed to me that he had wandering eyes, but my husband always said he was such a great guy. I look over his shoulder, to see how long it will be before Meerkat Christina clocks his praying mantis routine. Yep, right on cue; here she comes.

"Stephanie, darling!" Christina Wachman bursts between Greg, Giovanna, Alejandro and me like an anorexic, over-excited Labrador. "Sorry, I was distracted back there," she says, glaring at Greg.

"So, how is everything going with your music?" Christina says, with the merest hint of a sneer. "I saw on your Instagram that you were featured in the *Gay Times* this month. Great picture. Fabulous."

I open my mouth to respond, but she cuts me off: "It's just so interesting that the gays love you so much, isn't it?" She looks at Alejandro, pointedly. "Don't you think, Alejandro?"

"It's probably because both she AND the music are fantastic..." he says, sharply.

Christina continues: "Yes, why is that? Do you think the straight community doesn't get your music, Stephanie?"

Really? This schtick AGAIN?

Okay, I have to admit that I'm not known for my subtlety. Last term's school talent show (Logan was playing the guitar) unfortunately clashed with a Gay Pride performance, but, me being me, I was determined to do both. After headlining on Reading's main stage, Jan put the pedal to the metal to get me back to the school. I turned up about twenty minutes after the show had started, and bolted so fast up the auditorium's centre stairs that I dropped my iPhone, during a silent transition between acts. Everyone turned around when it bounced down half a flight of steps, and saw that I was not only wearing gold-sequinned hotpants (and the kind of heels that would make a drag queen wince), but the Gay Pride rainbow flag was emblazoned on one butt cheek.

I'd say that we are almost half a century into Pride now and, to be honest, who actually differentiates between gay and straight anymore? And, while I do have a lot of fans who are gay – including the school's fabulous head of drama, who emailed me last week to ask me if I'd judge next year's talent show – that's not really the point. The point is the music; giving joy to ALL the people who like to dance, whoever they choose to love. Sometimes – and certainly in cases like this – I feel far more at home on stage, performing in front of thousands, than being in the company of my "friends".

"I guess they just love a bit of glitz and glam! They like to let loose and have fun," I say to Christina, choosing to not let my heckles be raised.

"Still, so amazing you manage to fit it all in – you know, around the family. Especially now, after..." Christina doesn't finish the sentence. "I just wouldn't be able to do it. You must be *soooo* busy. Especially with the fundraiser coming up."

Christina is talking about the P.T.A. fundraiser, where we're raising money to build a whole new school, in a remote part of Nepal. We're hosting it at Café Michael.

"Yes, thank you SO much for letting us host it at the restaurant, Steph," Christina says. "We are SO grateful."

"Oh, my absolute pleasure."

I can feel my phone buzzing again in my purse. Franz. For the third bloody time!

Are you going to take that? I think you should – my husband's voice is ever-present in my head again.

Oy vey. Really?

Take the call, babe.

"Would you excuse me for a moment?" I say to the group, gesturing to the phone. I go through a side archway, into the corridor, and see tall French doors leading onto a terrace. As I leave, I see Christina immediately take Greg by the arm and lead him away into a corner, to scold him. No doubt she will save the real punishment for later. It's cold outside. Freezing, in fact.

"Hi, Franz," I say, shivering. "Sorry I missed your calls."

"Steph, where have you been?"

"Erm, at my gig and now a party. It's late, Franz; you never call – what's up?"

"Well…" Franz begins, "I need to discuss some things with you…"

A few minutes later, all I can manage to say is: "Oh, God!"

I was sweating profusely in the zero-degree weather, but now I am shaking with the cold – chilled to the bone and completely dazed.

I know I've got to go back inside, but I'm not sure which is worse: freezing my tuchas off on Christina Wachman's balcony, or going back inside and pretending that everything's fine, when I've just been told that the restaurants I depend on for financial survival have dived to the bottom of the failure pit, and won't survive another quarter.

But this is all part of the Chelsea Two-Step: always look like a swan, elegantly gliding through the water; don't EVER let ANYONE see the frantic paddling underneath. Even when the shit has well and truly hit the fan.

Alejandro, Christina, Gio, Pietro and Amanda are still talking and laughing when I eventually return to the party. I swipe a glass of wine from a passing waiter's tray and slip into the circle next to Alejandro, where the group is laughing at a story Christina is telling, about the last time they went to St. Barth's.

"And then you just CANNOT imagine what happened when the lobster arrived!" she says, clutching at her throat and bending over in laughter. Loud guffaws. I join in.

"All okay, hun?" Alejandro says in my ear.

"Yes, fine, fine." I see the glass I picked up on the way over is already empty. "Yes. All good. Do you know what? I think I'll have another glass of wine."

I don't sleep well that night: toss, turn, repeat. Over and over again, I keep running through what Franz told me on the phone. Café Michael is in huge financial trouble; it has simply not recovered from the pandemic, like a gazillion other hospitality businesses. Without a significant and speedy bailout (unlikely, in Franz's view), both restaurants will have to close, people will lose their jobs, and our family…? Well, we won't have a secure income. A paid singing gig from time to time helps, but it doesn't pay all bills that demand my attention every month.

"Hold up," I'd said to Franz on the phone, "you're telling me there is nothing? Surely there is some backup? Surely that can't be it? What? Poof? All gone?! And, what the actual fuck: you guys just let me spend a ton on renovations?!"

I recently invested a serious amount of the previous year's profits on a revamp of the London restaurant. It was a chance to stay ahead of the competition, when dining out got back into full swing. And it looks totally amazing! Everyone says so.

But, according to Franz, confidence and Café Michael have

never really recovered from all the isolating, quarantining and mandatory shutdowns.

Plus, the fallout from that sorry episode with the prawns...

He was referring to a particularly dreadful weekend last year, when not one but two celebrities got food poisoning at the New York flagship: dodgy langoustines.

Franz told me that, indeed, there is not much left, and it was his advice that I would have to put the company into administration.

I reach over for my phone. Five a.m. Time to get up and figure this shit out.

In the shower, the steaming water running over my neck and shoulders, and down my back, is so hot that it makes me wince. We all know that businesses have suffered in recent times, but is Café Michael really in THAT bad of a shape?! The last financial statements weren't exactly glowing, as I remember, and the small investors weren't fantastically pleased, but I don't recall anyone sounding emergency klaxons.

'Sides, Franz is our "guy"; he pretty much runs the day-to-day. That really isn't my thing, to be honest. And I thought we'd managed to dodge the bullet when we closed during the pandemic; I remember that Franz used the furlough schemes and government grants... I must have some emails somewhere?

I turn off the shower. The warmth dissipates. My shoulders

still ache. I reach for a towel.

I mean, the London flagship was buzzing the other day, when we had the P.T.A. meeting. They loved the new breakfast, and the new steak sauce I concocted with Rudolf, the new Swiss chef. The chic, fresh décor made everything perfect. They couldn't wait to host the Nepal fundraiser there!

Oh, God. The fundraiser.

Is that mole a problem? My dead husband appears and leans against the bathroom door.

THE MOLE? I say. *Don't you mean the restaurants? Because they seem to be a big problem right now!* I rub away the condensation on the bathroom vanity mirror, so that I can inspect the brownish splotch on my left shoulder. He's been going on about that mole for months. Is it getting any bigger? Maybe a little. It still looks pretty small to me.

Hey, don't sweat the restaurants. Get that mole checked out, he says. *Why don't you go see Dr. Stern? And, I have to say, Steph, I REALLY love the remix on the new single. It's gonna do so well out there, babe.*

"Don't sweat the restaurants?!" I say out loud. "Those restaurants are our life! Your legacy!"

My High Performing Husband – or "H.P.H.", as we always half-jokingly called my late spouse – really did spend his life on a high-performing run. Café Michael started out small, as a local bistro in New York: Tribeca, to be exact. H.P.H. was a connoisseur of great food and incredible wine, and slowly turned this passion into a thriving business. The first Café Michael was the place to "see and be seen" in the Big Apple. It didn't hurt that it launched with a celebrity chef from Chicago: Michael Schmitt, after whom the original restaurant was named. Then we moved to London and opened one there.

The restaurants served great food and were famous for their vibe. The Chelsea one was a huge deal on the London scene. Celebrities hung out there; people celebrated their birthdays and anniversaries there; boyfriends proposed to their girlfriends over our tables; there were endless business lunches, after-work dinners and, yes, even P.T.A. fundraisers. Café Michael is The Place. Correction: *was* the place.

If I close the restaurants, what does that mean? How are we meant to live now? How am I meant to pay the school fees? Or the staff? And, if I can't – if Team Steph really has to go – how on Earth am I going to tell them?

Down in the kitchen, Beverly is getting breakfast ready.

"Good morning," she trills. "Up so early, even with the concert and that posh party last night?"

My Irish nanny is, as usual, wearing a cardigan and a broad smile, sashaying between the sink and the table, armed with bowls and cutlery. She goes back to the counter and pours me a coffee. "What a workhorse you are! Well, here's to another fantastic day."

Fantastic? I smile the biggest stage smile I can manage and take the cup, feeling like I want to puke.

We hired Beverly a few years back – a little over a year before my husband died, actually. It happened at a time when my music career really started to take off; when I'd had to quickly learn how to balance performances with touring, radio appearances, travel schedules, my kids' exams, football matches, dance classes, school plays, P.T.A. meetings… oh, and being a great wife, of course. My mom had been helping out, but that took its toll, because she couldn't stay in London all the time to help me with the kids; my father was ill and he needed care. Then, when he died… well, that situation didn't work, either. We needed a professional. I wasn't sure about having a "live-in" nanny, but my husband was right: although my mother was great, it wasn't fair to rely on her. With our work schedules and the kids' logistics, a professional was kinda necessary.

I was relieved that my H.P.H. supported my ambition to become a recording artist, even though it was a huge shift from being at home full-time with the kids, and especially with all the pressures of him running a restaurant business. The restaurants were doing well, though, so we could certainly afford the extra set of hands. I just dreaded hiring a stranger – particularly if that stranger was going to live in the house with us. Part of me felt guilty. What if the kids hated the idea? And, even worse, hated me because of it? Another part of me felt ashamed that I even needed help. It felt like I wasn't able to cope with everything on my plate anymore.

Then there was the largest part of me, which felt scared that I might not find anyone who fit the bill. I interviewed a lot of nannies, hired a few and subsequently fired them. In desperation, I placed a small ad for a "professional live-in nanny" in a swanky London magazine.

When Beverly frickin' Poppins walked in, she stood out like a ray of sunshine on a dark, stormy day. She was hope and calm – all that good stuff you want when you have three children, all with their own needs, a High Performing Husband, a busy Chelsea social life, P.T.A. duties, and a contract to play weekly at The Pink Coconut, as well as various other clubs and Pride festivals around Europe.

When Beverly arrived for the interview, I was trying to work our new coffee machine. She immediately stepped in, and I watched her seamlessly figure out the coffee pods and the milk frother, even asking me if I wanted soymilk. Twenty seconds later, two immaculate cups of soy cappuccino were presented on the kitchen bar. In that moment, I knew that this tall, proud woman, from some small town outside of Galway, was exactly who I needed.

With her curly-set, auburn hair and neat pearl earrings, to her M&S cardigans and broad, kind smile, she couldn't have been farther from, or more detached from, the dance music and L.G.B.T.Q. scene with which I was getting deeper involved. But somehow our friendship and respect for each other transcended all this. She seemed to understand where I was in my life, and why what I was doing was so important. She understood how conflicted I was about juggling family and a blossoming career, and was hugely supportive when I lost my husband, helping me through the grief. She seemed to understand that the music was carrying me forward, even though I'd lost so much. And the brilliant thing about Beverly was she never once made me feel like a bad mother for doing it.

"You must, *must* follow your dreams, Stephanie," she would say, as she folded the kids' clothes or packed their lunches. "Of course, my generation didn't have the opportunities," she also liked to say, as I was rushing around preparing for a recording session or a Gay Pride event. "But yours does, and you must seize the opportunities with both hands. And you must not feel one moment of any guilt about doing so, my love."

Beverly was so wise and generous, offering advice and taking the time to really get to know my kids, with all their quirks and needs. She'd come with immaculate references, too; both the doctor couple with three kids, and the single mom of twins, who Beverly worked for previously, raved about her. They all told me she was an "angel from Heaven"; I'd found a real-life Mary Poppins.

Beverly is more than a nanny; she is Chief Operating Officer

– a true mother's help. But, most importantly, Beverly is my friend.

How the hell am I going to tell her that she can't stay?

I look into my coffee cup, hoping to find the answers there.

But then my assistant Candice bounds into the kitchen, like an excited terrier.

"Hey, Steph!" she says. "Hi, Bev!"

Seriously, Candice is amazing: young and beautiful, with a sunny, easy-going, South African disposition. Sure, she was very young and a little bit green when she officially started working as my husband's assistant, but she was sparky, and quickly transitioned from being one of Café Michael's beautiful hostesses, just barely out of high school – taking reservations and showing people to their table – to handling all of his (and now mine and the families) travel arrangements and diary management. And now liaising with Tony, arranging meetings and appointments, and joining me on tour. It's probably best if we just brush over the bit when my eldest kid discovered via Google that she had appeared on the South African version of *Big Brother*, before she moved over to London, and subsequently posed topless for a bunch of lads' mags, but she is super fun. She is a junior member of Soho House, and has a lot of friends in the music and T.V. biz. She's truly fabulous. The problem is that I can't see her staying around if there's no pay packet.

"So, your mother is leaving on her cruise tomorrow," says Candice, immediately getting out her phone. "We still need to pay the balance on that; I think we must have just overlooked it. Shall I do that for you?"

Shit! The cruise! Ten nights in a suite on the H.M.S. Sunshine. The pre-Covid seventieth birthday present I'd gifted my mother and her new boyfriend, Gerald Fortman, an eighty-something former plastic surgeon from Florida who, like my mother, recently buried his spouse in a sunny cemetery on the other side of the Atlantic. They met in the elevator of her apartment building when Gerald was visiting his cousin, who lives in the same complex as my mom. She later confided in me that she had seen him before on J-Date, the Jewish dating app, but had originally swiped left.

"Good morning, Stephanie," says Jan, sauntering into the kitchen. *Jan is up? At this time?* It's like they know something is up. He pulls up a chair in the nook and starts chatting to Candice.

Logan walks in and grabs a banana from the fruit bowl, closely followed by Emily.

Jeezy…! Well, that's it; I absolutely can't talk to the staff about the money now.

"Can I get some cereal, please, Mom?" asks Emily.

I pour the Rice Krispies into Emily's favourite bowl, and mimic Gio's Italian accent: "That's '*may* I have some cereal, please'."

Giovanna is trying to teach Emily "princess manners", and she loves it when Gio tells her stories about growing up and learning how to act like a royal. Em diligently picks up her spoon and says in a sing-song voice: "May I have some cereal, *pleeeease?*"

I laugh and smile warmly at my daughter. The kids have all done so well since their father died, they really have. Sometimes I look at them and am just utterly amazed at their resilience.

"Okay, so, the cruise... how much is the balance?" I ask Candice, as casually as I can manage, trying to stop nervously tapping my coffee cup.

"Erm..." Candice says, scrolling through her phone, "let me find the email... Right, okay, here it is: ten nights on the H.M.S. Sunshine, Riviera Suite for two, all-in... fifteen-thousand U.S. dollars." Then she adds: "Room service and spa treatments are extra."

$15,000?! I must have been mad! Surely there are better deals out there now to go on a cruise?

"The balance after the deposit is ten grand," says Candice. "Should I just use the credit card, or do you want to sort it with the bank?"

I absolutely love my mother (even though, like all mothers, she can be a teensy bit annoying), and she absolutely deserves a once-in-a-lifetime cruise – she's only just got back on track after the death of my father – but $15,000?! Oy vey! I mean, what was I smoking when I booked this? I am NOT Christina Wachman.

"Stephanie? You didn't answer the question?" says Candice, waving her palm in front of my eyes. "What am I doing about the cruise bill: bank or credit card? You'll get tonnes of air miles with the credit card."

Like I'm going to be flying anywhere soon.

"Sure, stick it on the credit card," I say, trying to sound as nonchalant as possible. "You're absolutely right about the air miles. Good thinking, Candice." I punch her playfully on the arm, secretly praying that it doesn't take the Amex over the limit. I'm really going to need to get a grip on this.

It's fine, it's all fine… I say in my head, over and over again. *I can do this.* I'll just sort that out later. I'm definitely not sacking them all now.

Chapter 2

"You Give Me Everything"

ONE WEEK LATER...
THURSDAY NIGHT.

"Seriously?" Alejandro says, taking a large gulp from his can of M&S G-and-T, and reaching for a packet of Twiglets on the arm of the crappy dressing-room sofa. "You really have to shut the restaurant?"

"Restaurants," I say, breathlessly; "remember, we have two."

It's eleven p.m., and I've just come off stage at The Pink Coconut, breathless and schvitzing for England. It has been a GREAT gig – one of my best so far. The crowd went crazy – so wild, in fact, that I found myself stage-diving at the end of the first set, and literally surfed the crowd while they were all chanting the chorus to my latest single.

So many friends and fans were in the club tonight, including Bazza, the promoter who booked me on my first Gay Pride tour across the U.K., and Gary, the part-time model and loyal bar manager at Café Michael in London, who is always bigging up my latest releases. In fact, he texted me earlier today: *"Heard your new song playing on Gaydio Radio this morning! Sooooo amazing, darling. I couldn't help but dance my way into the shower!"* Alejandro, Beaver and Tony were also all there, elevating me above everyone else in the room, passing me overhead, from person to person – literally lifting me up and supporting me. I'd never felt happier or more alive.

"Yeah, cut and run before it's too late – that's what Franz says." I grab a hand towel and wipe the sweat from my face and neck, leaving marks of dark-brown bronzer on it. I'm still high on adrenaline, able to talk about Café Michael without bursting into tears – and, given that I've only confessed to Al so far, this is probably a good thing. I flash him a look at the towel and giggle: "Yuck, eh?"

"Oh, wow, the glamour!" Alejandro laughs. "Here, have a gin, darling."

I take the can of gin and tonic, and snap back the ring pull. Then I slump onto the sofa next to him.

"I'm not going to let this get the better of me, you know... this restaurant crap. I'm going to fix it. I'm not killing off K.C.'s hard work; I'm going to find a solution."

"Course you will, Steph," he says, putting his arm around me. "But have your gin first, sweet pea. Gin makes everything better."

I'm not sure about that, but it tastes pretty good. I take another slug.

Franz – who flits between London and New York – and I had now had hour upon hour of conversations with the management team at the London restaurant, crunching the numbers and thinking through various scenarios. There doesn't ever seem to be a good answer, though; the restaurants are heavily in debt. Although they are buzzing on some nights, financial confidence hasn't fully returned. Like so many others, what my husband and I have built up looks like it is about to become yet another statistic in the "Failed Medium-Sized Businesses" column.

There have also been depressing chats with my financial advisor.

"No restaurants equals no income. You won't be able to afford the school fees," he told me, bluntly. Followed by: "You certainly can't keep the staff. As for staying in the house – well, that's fifty-fifty; there is still a mortgage to pay. The bottom line is – and I don't delight in telling you this, Mrs. Bloom – your life is about to change, in all sorts of major ways."

The financial advisor almost laughed when I suggested that now my music – the thing I've been desperate to pursue for so long – might hold the answer if I really pushed it… and he seriously never laughs at anything.

"Mrs. Bloom, forgive me," the financial advisor told me, "but your concerts at The Pink Coconut don't bring in anywhere near enough to sustain your family or your lifestyle.

Downloads, tours and merchandise in general help a bit, but it's
– forgive me once more – just a tiny piss in the pot."

"So, you're serious?" Alejandro asks. "You're going to stop
all this?"

Am I?

"Ugh, not now, Al. I really do not want to discuss this."

"I mean, did you SEE all those people tonight? The ones
chanting your name? Carrying you across the room? It was
incredible!"

"A few fans in London chanting my name ain't gonna pay
the mortgage, babe."

"But you've worked so hard! It's more than a hobby, Steph!
If that were all it was, you would have taken up golf, for
Chrissake! You've got real fans, had ACTUAL hit records…!
It's only a matter of time…"

I shake my head, both to tell Alejandro to stop talking and
try to stop the tears from starting up again.

"I have to put this on the back burner. I have to focus on
the restaurant, Al, for the kids. The restaurants can make a lot
more profit than this does."

Make? Made.

Who am I kidding? In truth, as far as Franz is concerned,
the restaurants are already flatlining and have a D.N.R. order on
them.

"Well, maybe you can do both," Alejandro says, not giving

up, offering me an open packet of Twiglets.

"Nah, thanks." I push away the packet, smiling weakly.

"No to the Twiglet, or no to doing both?"

"Al, stop, *please!* It's serious. H.P.H. and I built those restaurants from scratch! It was his dream and I supported him. I can't just let that go…"

I stare at the picture on my cell phone next to me, and whisper under my breath: "I *can't* let you go." I still haven't managed to change the screensaver on my phone: an old photo of H.P.H. and I taken at the London launch of Café Michael. The two of us have the broadest of smiles, holding champagne flutes with the *"C.M."* insignia on them. My nails were painted royal blue, to match his favourite soccer team, Chelsea F.C.

"But, what about all the new deals Tony's got going? That other guy who turned up tonight seemed like a big deal."

"A few podcast appearances and a couple of bigger gigs up north is not going to put bread on the table. It's sure not going to pay the mortgage, either."

"I dunno, Steph. When I was talking to him in the bar, it didn't sound like just a few podcasts…" says Alejandro.

"Oh, COME ON, AL. We've been here SO MANY TIMES! Remember when he said he'd got me on *Strictly*? I'm not holding my breath."

Hang on: what other guy? Tony never mentioned another guy.

Feeling completely deflated, I bury my head into my best friend's chest, and he wraps his arms around me.

"Come on, sweetie," Alejandro says, with a wry smile, "it's late. We both know you've got the school P.T.A. meeting tomorrow, and I also know that you haven't listened to that financial advisor of yours and sacked the driver yet, because I saw Jan throwing peanuts in his mouth at the bar. It'll all work out, sweetie. No rash decisions. Now, let's go home."

"Did you hear?" says Amanda May conspiratorially, the next afternoon. Leaning across her skinny cappuccino in Café Michael, we are waiting for the P.T.A. meeting to begin. "The Langhams are in a bit of a bind. Pandemic totally screwed Rod's business. They've let their chef go *and* the live-in cleaner. But now I also heard that it's got so bad they may have to pull the kids out of school and send them to…" she wrinkled her nose, "the local state."

"Oh, my goodness. Poor things."

"I know. Anyway, I know we've all taken a bit of a hit, but thank God that's not *our* lives, HAHAHA! State school? Imagine!"

My heart is beating wildly. *Not our lives? Oy vey!*

I look over at the bar and spot Gary. He looks morose, compared to the joy I saw on his face last night at The Pink

Coconut. Standing behind the counter, head down, slowly wiping down the bar, it is not Gary at all. *Oy...* And if Gary knows, then pretty much everyone else is about to know, as well. *Shit.*

"Would you excuse me?" I say to Amanda, getting up and heading in the direction of the bar.

I look around as I walk across the room, and I have to say that the restaurant looks absolutely stunning. It's quite busy today, with various locals sitting at the highly-polished mahogany tables. The white bone-china plates I had shipped from Milan and the silver chargers look amazing. Heavy silver salt and pepper shakers. Cut-glass crystal. Turn-of-the-century elegance juxtaposed with a modern vibe. Super cute. I admit, I did spend quite a lot of money on the redecoration. And I'm actually quite pissed that they let me do it at all, since the finances were in such bad shape. On the other hand – as Al put it, the night before – when a place looks this good, how can it even be allowed to fail?

"Hey, Gar!" I say cheerily, when I get to the bar. "How's it going?!"

"Oh, hey, Steph," he says flatly, continuing to look downward. "Great gig last night. You were awesome, and that was some epic crowd surfing! I'm not doing too bad. What can I get you?"

"Erm, skinny cappuccino, please. Just waiting for the fancy-schmancy school mommies to turn up," I say, trying to lighten the mood, and nodding over to the table where a couple more have just sat down.

I decide to tackle Gary head-on. "You're not your usual self, babe," I say.

Gary has the worst poker face; he cracks immediately. "Oh, man, Steph… I mean, I know it's been hard… we've all known the world's been utterly screwed, and I know I'm lucky to even still have a job here. But," he leans across the counter and whispers, "the truth is, we haven't been paid in *weeks*. The chef went nuts the other day, because the guys at head office told him he couldn't order the same organic meat. They're cutting costs everywhere. There's a leak in the ladies' bathroom and no one has fixed it. Someone said the same stuff is going on in New York. It's just… well, it's just awful."

I look down at the floor. If this place closes, Gary and so many others are going to be on the unemployment line.

"I know," I say. "Well, I didn't know, but I do now."

Gary looks at me, his eyes wide with worry. He reaches across the counter and grabs my hands. "Is it the end? Can you do something?"

I sigh: "Gary, babe, I promise you, I'm working on it."

There are always rumours in Chelsea: who is sleeping with whom, who is rich, who is less rich, who is gaining, who is losing, whose marriage is on the rocks, whose kids are taking drugs or being bullied… In a part of London where appearances are everything, I know I have to keep this under control. I look around me; I can see other members of staff in the room, watching us. The internal rumour mill has already started. It is only a matter of time before it gets out.

A tidal wave of nausea bolts through me and I begin to feel sick. Puke sick. I excuse myself and head downstairs to the bathrooms, lock myself in a cubicle, then immediately start to throw up. After a few minutes, my stomach is empty and my throat stings. I put the toilet seat down and collapse onto it.

I have faith in you, Steph, H.P.H. says in my head. *What is it Emily says? Something like: "When life hands you lemons... you make orange juice"?*

Ya, I say, remembering her response when I asked her what she meant: "You just gotta be creative, Mom."

He's gone again. That's the problem with ghosts: they just pop in and out, like they're not really properly there anymore. It's hard to believe anything they say, frankly.

I catch my reflection in the full-length mirror, on the way out of the bathroom stall. Rough. Like I've just gone a few rounds with Mike Tyson. I remove my make-up bag from my purse, quickly touch up my eyeliner and slap on some lip gloss. Then, as I reach inside my bag, feeling for a box of Tic-Tacs, to take the taste of the vomit out of my mouth, I notice my phone flashing: a text from Tony.

"HEY, S, DO YOU FANCY BOSTON?"

Oy, he's got the phone stuck on caps lock again.

"Birmingham?" I type back.

Huh, yeah, we've actually done a few gigs up there, haven't we? Central England, somewhere near Leeds, I think. Honestly, I found it hilarious, when we first moved over here, that a lot of the places in the States I knew so well were actually named after places in England. I mean, I guess it's obvious; what else were the English settlers going to call their new homes? But it was funny when I found myself at Brighton Pride, talking to people who'd come from Newhaven, and I was like: "Whoa, Newhaven, Connecticut?" And they were like: "Er, no, Newhaven about thirty minutes down the coast."

"BIG DEAL! BOSTON: YES OR NO?" Tony texts back.

"Sure," I type back, not really concentrating, *"Boston's fine. In a meeting. Call you later."*

I slip the phone back in my bag, finally find the pack of Tic-Tacs, throw a couple in my mouth and bolt back upstairs.

"Sorry, ladies, had to take a call," I say, slipping into my seat and noticing that my shoes, drenched from the leaky toilet water, have been making marks all across the polished parquet floor. Everyone is sipping on their drinks or stirring in sweetener, and I see that Gary has put a cappuccino on the table, in front of my chair.

"Stephanie," Christina Wachman says, in full-on schoolteacher mode, "we've just been discussing the fundraiser. We just wanted to check the arrangements for taking over the café on the night."

"Right," I nod, uber-serious, hoping my poker face is better than Gary's.

"So, will it still be possible…" Christina pauses, "…to hold the event here, at the restaurant?"

Everyone around the table stares at me. Their eyes are boring into me. Shit.

"Er, well…" I begin, then my phone starts ringing again. Shit, left it on loud! Christina purses her lips, pissed.

"I am *so* sorry, ladies." I point to the phone, standing up again and hitting the green button. "I've really got to take this."

I don't want to have the conversation inside, so I head out, pushing open the restaurant's grand iron and glass doors, and hurry onto the street.

"Hi, Franz. Sorry, I was in a meeting."

"Franz? Who's Franz?" says the voice on the line, sounding like they are really not awake.

"Tony?"

"Hey, S, thought I'd call. You weren't responding to my texts."

"I said I was in a meeting, Tony!"

"Yeah. So, we're good to go with Boston?"

"Sure, Boston sounds fine. Talk later. Gotta run, babe," I say, distracted by another incoming call. As I'm about to hang up on Tony, I hear faintly: "I'll email Candice the details." Then, *click*.

The incoming call really is Franz this time, and I bet he's not in the mood for niceties. I hit the green icon.

"Hello," I say, like a nervous schoolgirl who just got caught wearing red nail polish to school.

"Stephanie, I really need to push you for an answer," Franz says, sternly. "Can I start to look for buyers? We can't go ahead without your say-so."

"Tell me again what it means. Is there really no other way?"

"We've been through this quite a few times now, Stephanie," he says, more than a little patronizingly. "It means that we sell both restaurants, then we pay off the debts, take stock and decide what to do next."

Don't get emotional, sweetie. The H.P.H. is in my head again. *It's just business.*

Not for me. This is personal.

I stare back up at Café Michael's grand façade. I really love this building. I always thought that the light sandstone, with its long windows, was a beacon against the darker, red-brick buildings in the street.

It was a beacon of light in so many ways: our second restaurant and a step on the road to H.P.H.'s ambitions of opening up more Café Michaels around the world. We made the move here after ten years in New York and, had the London restaurant not been successful, who knows what would have happened? I suppose we would have left London and gone back to the States, or maybe even Canada.

But, if we didn't stay, perhaps I wouldn't have had the opportunity to live my own musical dreams, writing and performing. This is where my career all started – at forty, no less. It felt like I was given a "reboot" when I was catapulted into the dance-music world – a scene typically reserved for youth, which is a lot more prominent in Europe and the U.K. than it has been in the U.S. So, it was an opportunity of a lifetime which I'm not so sure would have ever even happened had we left the U.K.

Staring at the C.M. logo on the door handles brings back memories of my young children doing their homework at the bar, and Gary making Emily her favourite smoothies (calling them "Emithies"). I remember all the gorgeous and elegant private parties which took place there, from weddings to bar mitzvahs, and red carpet and charity events. The King's Road venue framed my family's life in the U.K. This was the cornerstone of my husband's legacy.

And I am about to start chopping down that old oak tree…

I start to shake. I feel the tears stream down my cheeks. There is a hollowness in the pit of my stomach, as if someone hit the gravity switch and the entire planet has just dropped out from under my feet.

"Stephanie, you there? I really need an answer on this – like, yesterday," Franz says, annoyed.

"Franz, I'll have to call you back," I say, wiping the tears off my face. "I can't do this right now." I hit the red button.

"Sorry, ladies. My manager," I say, when I return to the table. "New gig. Up north. Needed to confirm."

Christina looks at me suspiciously. "Amazing how dedicated you are to your music – even with..." she says, letting her voice trail off.

And, in that moment, I snap:

"Sorry, Christina, you were asking me about the café on the night of the fundraiser?"

"Yes, we were just worried that maybe..."

"Maybe what?" I say, sharply. "Of course it's okay to hold the fundraiser here."

Oh, God, what am I saying?

"We just thought that—"

"You thought what, Christina?"

She purses her lips.

"Well?"

"Well, I think the ladies and I just wanted some kind of assurance..."

"Christina, I can assure you," I say, looking the Bitch of Belgravia straight in the eye, "the fundraiser will be taking place here."

The show MUST go on.

Somehow.

Chapter 3

"Thou Shalt Not Slay the Gays"

ONE WEEK LATER...

EN ROUTE TO HEATHROW.

"And then Tony say: 'Nooo, Steph, I meant Boston, *Massachusetts,*' and you say: '*WHAT?!*'" Jan chuckles in his heavy Polish accent, and thumps the steering wheel of the Range Rover. "I swear, I never forget your face when you realize. So funny, Steph! HA! HA! HA! HA! HA!" He throws his head back in fits of laughter, as we sit in traffic on the Hammersmith flyover, while he continues to recount how exactly we came to be going to Boston... the one on the other side of the Atlantic, not the one near Leeds.

"And Tony say: 'Don't be idiot, Steph. Why would MOST FAMOUS RAPPER IN THE WORLD be in Boston, Lincolnshire?'! Ha-ha-ha!"

Oh, completely freaking hilarious! I think, nervously fiddling with the cocktail rings on my fingers. I mean, no doubt I have a lot on my plate, but I have been living in London for many years now, and have performed all over the U.K., in places like Birmingham and Portsmouth. And, when Tony books gigs for me in those places, I don't immediately think he means Birmingham, Alabama, or Portsmouth, Rhode Island, do I? So why the heck would I have thought Tony meant Massachusetts when it came to Boston? I mean, c'mon, I'm practically a Brit now.

"What time is the flight again?" I ask Candice, who is sitting next to me in the back, and still looks the teeniest bit uncomfortable about the mix-up. I haven't told her I'm pissed that she booked us both business-class seats without checking with me, mostly because the staff are still in the dark about my current financial situation. But, put it this way: that Amex – and the emergency Mastercard – must be within kissing distance of the limit now.

"Er, three p.m. take-off," says Candice. Then she leans in and whispers: "I really am sorry, Steph. Tony said to book it. I honestly didn't know you thought it was just a gig up the M1."

On the one hand, I could absolutely murder Tony right now. On the other... well, I could frankly kiss him. Which would be fine, considering I'm a widow, but also seriously gross and inappropriate.

"It's okay, babe," I say to Candice, "don't sweat it. It's a crazy opportunity."

"Recording with the world's leading rap music artist? I should say it is," says Jan. "Opportunity of the century!"

See? Told you that you had to go, I hear H.P.H. say in my head.

Alejandro said the same, of course ("No, Steph, you're going!"). And even Giovanna, initially suspicious of me recording with a "rapper", has given the trip her royal blessing. Beaver is super-excited to be on the team, and agreed to be paid half his usual rate because he's in the States already, which is good, because I also have to fork out for the film crew who are coming with us, to document everything and get footage for the music video. Even H.P.H. was egging me to book us into Boston's very expensive Lenox Hotel, because that's where Tony said we needed to be.

Expensive, honey, but necessary. Got to have skin in the game, he said, as I pressed the *"Pay now"* button. Do the dead just not care about debt?

So, it's a done deal: fly to Boston, meet THE MOST FAMOUS RAPPER IN THE WORLD, do a day of recording in the studio and then return to London. Franz has reluctantly agreed to hold fire on announcing the sale-slash-closure of the restaurants 'til I get back. I'm also thinking that, if I can stall him for a bit longer, it might just mean I get away with being able to hold the P.T.A. fundraiser at Café Michael without losing face, as well. And, thinking SUPER-positively, although the schedule is tight, with a fair wind I could even zip down to New York, see my kid and meet with Café Michael's head office, to get the scoop in person.

That's my girl, says H.P.H. in my head, as the car speeds down the M4. *You always come up with the goods.*

"We here, Steph," Jan says in his Polish lilt, stopping the car at the drop-off-and-pick-up point, and switching on the hazard lights. "Let me get door for you."

I step onto the pavement and wait for Jan to bring round the bags, when I notice two extremely good-looking men start pointing at me and Candice, who is now wrestling with a luggage trolley. I look at them quizzically. They move closer and I hear one of them say: "Yeah, she's defo famous."

I can't resist saying something. "Me?" I say, shaking my hair. "Oh, well, just a little," I giggle. "In fact, I'm just off to—"

"Oh, nah, love, we meant your daughter." One of the men nods at Candice. My daughter?! Seriously? How old does he think I am? I feel myself turning bright red, then realize these guys probably could have seen Candice online or in a lad's mag, like my kids did.

"Er…"

"OF COURSE, *SHE'S* THE FAMOUS ONE! YOU BUFFOON!" comes a voice from behind. I look up and see a statuesque figure in shiny, pink Lycra bounding toward us. It's Lady Laura, M.C. at The Pink Coconut – one of Soho's most flamboyant transvestites and one of my most devoted fans. She bows theatrically to me, before addressing the two men.

"This, sir, is the most amazing Star Roberts, the GREATEST dance music star the world has EVER seen."

"Cool," says one of the men, while the other snaps a few photos on his phone.

Lady Laura turns to me: "Darling, how could we not come and wave you off to *Am-eri-ca?*" He sings the word, like the line in *West Side Story.* "I didn't sleep a wink last night! I am *sooooooo* excited for you, girl!"

Lady Laura motions behind her, and I see a group of ten or twelve of my most loyal fans all heading my way, including promoter Bazza! They are waving and whooping. Some are holding Star Roberts placards and masks. *Wow.* I posted on Instagram that I was going to the States, but didn't expect this; it's like a mini Star Roberts Mardi gras! The group throngs around me, excitedly.

"O.M.G., O.M.G., O.M.G.," trills Bazza. "Do you know, I totally love your look today! O.M.G., you've GOT to take a picture with me!"

He picks up his phone and extends it on a selfie stick. I lean into him and purse my lips. "Hashtag 'I'm with Star'!" he yells.

Huh, well, I suppose I do look quite good, as I smooth my leather trousers over my thighs.

"So, who," asks Lady Laura, "is the lucky D.J. you're working with this time? I bet you're reworking 'Band of Gold'! I *looooove* that track! Is it true that Samantha Ronson and Seth Gold both wanted to work with you? Or is it D.J. GayRay? I read on DanceFreak.com he was super-interested." *DanceFreak* is a blog in London. I hosted their annual awards ceremony last year.

"Erm…" another fan butts in, "NOOOOOO. I heard Star is up for a cameo for *C.S.I. Miami.*"

"No," says another, "that's not right. I read she's going to get her own cooking show." He nods knowingly. "With Ina Garten."

Ina Garten – now THERE is a gay-friendly cookery titan. Huh, not a bad idea… you know, if I could actually *cook*. I can't boil an egg, although my mother-in-law did once let me in on her secret to making the world's fluffiest Matzah balls. Apparently, it's all about the seltzer water.

Thankfully, Beverly is a master in the kitchen. The kids love her English pies and casseroles, so I'm absolutely not worried about her looking after Logan and Emily while I'm away.

"Guys, guys, guys," I say, outstretching my palms, as if I were trying to calm a bunch of overexcited toddlers, "none of you have it right!" The group stops bickering and falls silent. Ha-ha! Now I have their attention. "It's soooo much bigger, soooo much better than any of that." I pause for dramatic effect. "The truth is, I'm going to BOSTON to record with THE MOST FAMOUS RAPPER IN THE WORLD!"

Complete and utter silence.

Ewww, the mood of the Star Roberts Mardi Gras Five has just totally bombed. Like a bad night at The Pink Coconut, when the A.V. system breaks down and everyone's drunk on rum cocktails already.

"Guys, come on! Isn't that great?" I say again, eyes wide, both palms outstretched. "THE MOST FAMOUS RAPPER IN THE WORLD!"

More silence. What have I done? I stare at Lady Laura in desperation. Laura has always backed me. She knows the challenges of working this niche.

Laura sees that I'm freaking out and immediately jumps to my defence. "Well, that's fantastic, Star! AMAZING! THE MOST FAMOUS RAPPER IN THE WORLD? Whoa, yeah! It's your time, babe!" She wiggles her hips and shakes her head, slightly changing up the chorus of one of my songs, "I Am a Woman". He sings:

"She is a woman, and she knows what she wants! Ya!"

Some of the guys join in and the atmosphere mellows a little, becoming a little more party-like once more.

"She is a woman, and she knows what she wants! Yaaaa! Feed her the rhythm!

"She is a woman, and she knows what she wants, ya… and all she wants is…"

"All she wants is to turn her back on US!!" Bazza chants loudly, cutting them all off.

"Hey, Baz!" Lady Laura says, hands on hips. "Come on. Just because Star is recording with a famous rapper, it doesn't mean she's turning her back on us. She's not dissing the scene. She's just moving on up."

Bazza isn't having any of it. "She's dumping us!" he says. "So, you know what? I'm dumping her! T.T.Y.N., Star!" He walks off and, in a huff, dumps his Star Roberts mask in the nearest bin.

"Hey, c'mon, guys, leave her alone," says Jan, puffing up his chest and barging through, to stand in front of me. "Let Star get her flight." Jan takes my arm and hustles me into the terminal building.

By the time Candice and I get to check-in, I'm beyond dazed. It's slightly unnerving how angry Bazza seems to be about all this. He really has gone to bat for me as a promoter, and really fought to get me the best slots in the early days. Oh, God, I feel like I've told him I robbed his house and I'm not giving back his fake tan and Right Said Fred albums. I knew my fans liked my music and, you know, maybe they even liked me, but I was never convinced that they cared all that much. I thought they just liked the upbeat songs and the hot young dancers I brought with me. Hey, maybe they liked the glittery costume, as well. I mean, why does it matter to them if I go mainstream? I can still come back and play The Pink Coconut! Why aren't they happy for me?

We haul the cases onto the conveyor belt and hand over our passports to the check-in clerk. Then I flash her my Star

Roberts smile. "Are we all set?" I ask Candice, as the clerk checks our passports, tickets and baggage tags.

Candice whips out the iPhone like a modern-day, trigger-happy sheriff: *swipe, swipe, swipe…*

"Erm, the D.J. for the fundraiser, Katsu, has sent you an email."

"Okay…"

Candice skim reads it out: "Er… okay, she's sent you her rider… So, she wants her own green room, fresh flowers, organic vegan snacks… And she says she's bringing Princess Fifi with her."

Ooh, the D.J. is bringing royalty to the Nepal School fundraiser. Nice. "Which royal family is Princess Fifi part of, I wonder?" I say. "I'll text Gio; she'll know."

Candice gives me her *"durrrrr"* look, cocking her head to one side. "It's her cat, Steph."

"Her CAT?"

"Yeah, Princess Fifi is a Siamese Blue Point."

Seriously? A cat? She can't bring a cat to Café Michael. Also, did no-one get the memo that I have a frickin' serious cat allergy?

"Okay!" I snap. "We'll formulate a response to D.J. Catwoman on the plane. Anything else?"

Candice, seeing that I am now in no mood to be messed with, quickly goes back to the iPhone.

"Well, there have been some pretty nasty tweets about you and THE MOST FAMOUS RAPPER IN THE WORLD! Most from... er... Bazza, by the looks of things.

"Okay, and... oh... there's something here from the film crew Tony booked. It says they can't come. They've got noro."

"What?" It takes a couple of seconds for this to compute.

"Norovirus. You know, the vomiting bug? They say they're really gutted," says Candice.

The check-in woman looks up from her desk. "I'm afraid your bags are quite significantly overweight, Mrs. Bloom," she says, smiling brightly. "How would you like to pay?"

As soon as we get onto the plane and into our seats, Candice puts on a black, silk eye-mask and falls asleep, staying in comatose mode most of the way to Boston. She misses out on the champagne and fillet steak, confirming my suspicion that she was partying late last night, after my show: The Box, probably. She went there with me to Rita Ora's birthday party last year.

I can't sleep. I'm too hyped and bothered by the incident with Bazza, which is still gnawing at me. I've already looked at his tweets: not nice. He's even included the picture we took, the one where he was being nice to me!

"@Bazzaspeaks:

"Just been at Heathrow with @StarRoberts. Found out that she is totally #betraying the #dancemusic #gay #scene recording with #mostfamousrapperintheworld #ttyn #horsesmouth."

Whoa!

And:

"@Bazzaspeaks:

"Always knew that she wasn't in it for her true fans. #noloyalty."

Yikes. Both of them have been retweeted, like, 2,000 times already. Not even a quick power nap is possible after reading that.

I decide to watch a film. I scroll through the myriad of offerings and settle on a choice of two: *Love, Actually* and *Straight Outta Compton* – I've got to do the rap thing, haven't I; go a bit "method"? I take a sip of my champagne, use the touchscreen to select the film, sit back and relax…

Then… absolutely freak out! There's already a police tank with a battering ram, and a drug bust and guns, and women being treated really freaking badly, in the first three minutes of the movie! And guns! Lots and lots of guns.

I hit stop, shut my eyes and try to rest. But I can't. I press play again and sit there for two-and-a-half hours, vaguely traumatized by the sheer brutality, racism and struggle which seemed to define the history of early gangsta rap. I find myself open-mouthed at the scene where the members of the N.W.A.

declare that gun violence is their truth. When the film is over, I gotta say I'm grateful for the other cosy stuff — like failing restaurants and the future financial stability of my family — racing around in my mind.

Chapter 4

"I'm A Bombshell"

We land in Boston on time. Outside, the sky is a deep slate colour and the captain tells us the air temperature outside is minus-three. Typical January East Coast weather. Fifty shades of grey misery.

Still, we're not here to go camping, are we? Nope, we're heading for a ritzy hotel that I can't afford. But I'm not going to think about that. At least, not now. I check my phone as we wait for the bags at the baggage carousel.

There's a waffling voicemail from my mother, which sounds like she is talking on the windy ship's balcony ("Lovely time on this cruise, darling. Thank you *soooo* much for your generosity! Gerald getting a tan and – hope you don't mind – I've treated myself to a few spa treatments, as well."). And a long string of messages on the P.T.A. WhatsApp group, discussing whether the auction should be silent and whether we should use the Café Michael charger plates for the fundraiser, or bring in something a bit more "glitzy". I chuck in a few thumbs-up emojis to show that I'm taking notice.

My son Zack has found me a replacement for my vomity

film crew, in the form of a couple of guys he knows from N.Y.U. Film School. He says they'll do it for their "work experience" portfolio if I pay for their flights and, oh yeah, "let them get stoned with the rapper."

"Got everything?" I ask, as Candice grabs the last of the bags off the conveyor belt. She makes a *"ta-da"* pose, as she manoeuvres the trolley stacked with suitcases toward me.

"Oh, yeah, baby!" she says, and smiles a broad showbiz smile.

"Great!" I say, before stopping in my tracks. "Candice, honey," I say, "before we go through customs, can I ask you a serious question?" The N.W.A. "Fuck Da Police" scene from *Straight Outta Compton* is still vividly embossed in my brain. "Not all rappers are dangerous, eh? Do you think we might be going into something where we should be... um, *concerned?*" I say, sounding so out of touch.

Candice appears to think about it for a second. "Nahhhhhh... course not. They're just into hip-hop, diamonds and flashy trainers. They're *soooo* cool, Steph! C'mon, let's go meet THE MOST FAMOUS RAPPER IN THE WORLD!"

You know what? She's totally right. And, as we head out into the arrivals hall, I feel as if I am walking on air. This is my time; I've waited years for this. So, whatever is going on back in London, for the next few days I'm going to forget about Franz and the financial advisor and the restaurant business and the P.T.A. moms and the fundraiser, and just concentrate on enjoying this. Because this is my time and it's going to be absolutely AMAZING.

"So, who are we meeting?" I say.

"Someone called Linus," says Candice, consulting her phone.

"Linus? As in the kid with the blanket in *Charlie Brown*?" I ask, remembering watching *Charlie Brown* and *Snoopy* cartoons snuggled up on the sofa with my brother, on Saturday mornings.

"Ummm, I guess." Candice is confused. "Yeah, like the kid in *Charlie Brown*."

In the arrivals hall, I see a tall, handsome and seriously fit guy, carrying a sign scrawled with: *"Boom"*. He's not really holding it – more dragging it around his waist.

"Mrs. Boom?" he says.

"Bloom, actually. Are you Linus?" I say.

"That's me, although they call me Lil' Li."

Lil' Li is not at all little; he is in fact about six-foot-four. He has a broad smile, diamond stud earrings and talks in short sentences, *veeerry* slowly, like he has all the time in the world. He wears an immaculate, white satin bomber jacket and grey baseball cap, and doesn't appear to be standing up straight. Maybe he just likes to slouch. I won't tell my kids about the slouching bit, I think; I don't want my kids to slouch, even if

Linus does manage to make it look really, really cool.

"I'm so excited!" I tell him, bouncing up and down. "Everything is set! Let's go and meet THE MOST FAMOUS RAPPER IN THE WORLD!"

Linus looks down, checking his phone. "He busy right now," he drawls.

"What?"

Silence. Linus doesn't look up.

I try again.

"Excuse me, but he's busy where?"

There is a pause and then Linus says: "We'll wait at the hotel."

"Okay. Great! Perfect!" I say. "So, I booked into the Lenox, as requested. I am ready. To. Rock. I mean: ready. To. Rap! Hahaha!"

Linus looks at me like I am an idiot.

"The Lenox? Nah, man, didn't your manager tell you? We goin' to Worcester."

"Worcester?" No, Tony did not tell me this.

"Yeah." He jerks his head in the direction of the exit. "Limo's outside."

Now, I have never been to Worcester, Massachusetts, but I do know that it is not the kind of place that has many hotels. Or shops. Or posh sushi restaurants. Or anything much, apart from a college campus and a few old mills. Also, and most importantly, THE MOST FAMOUS RAPPER IN THE WORLD is not meant to be in Worcester, Massachusetts. He is meant to be in downtown Boston, in the very expensive five-star hotel I can't really afford, waiting for my recording session of a lifetime. So, going to "God Knows Where" is NOT IN THE PLAN.

I glare at Candice. She shrugs and gives me her best "this-is-absolutely-not-my-fault" look, then digs around in her Michael Kors tote, pretending to be busy.

"Linus?" I say, hands on hips, forgetting for a moment the game plan to be extra nice at all times, because he is holding my future career in his hands... plus, I'm not quite sure of his political views on gun-toting. "It's all been arranged! The concert in Boston? The recording session? It's all been planned!" I say, over-anxiously.

"Sorry, lady," shrugs Linus with a quizzical look, still trying to suss me out, "plan's changed."

Should I call Tony? He made the arrangements. I look again at Linus and immediately decide against that idea. I suppose I could redirect Beaver? The film crew? I'll text Zack. Do I even have another option? The only saving grace, I suppose, is that I *might* be able to get my money back on the Lenox.

Candice is still avoiding my gaze, tapping away on her phone. I look back at Linus, who just shrugs and jerks his head, yet again, in the direction of the exit door.

I really don't have any choice, do I?

"Well, Linus," I sigh, "I guess Worcester it is."

As we sit in the back of the limo, driving out of the city, Linus tries to lighten the mood by showing me an elaborate handshake – a thing done by all members of THE MOST FAMOUS RAPPER IN THE WORLD'S posse, like a secret code. He grabs my hand and turns it palm-side up, sliding his palm down my palm, then twists it downward, to do the slide motion again against my palm; he then moulds my hands into a fist and pumps his fist onto mine. Seems simple enough.

"See that?" he drawls, slouching back in his seat, spreading his legs as wide as they could possibly go without being in an elaborate yoga pose.

I turn to Candice and the two of us try our best to copy what he's just shown me. I cock my head to one side, feeling like I've just been inducted into "da club". Huh, not so hard, really. I got this rapper stuff *down*, man. "Like this?" I say, proudly showing him the hand choreography with Candice. "Look, I got it!"

Linus looks at me with mild disdain. Then he says: "Nah, man, you ain't doing it right."

You really aren't getting it right, says the H.P.H., suddenly appearing next to me. *Look, watch me. And, honey, can you scoot over a bit?*

Okay, hold up, I think, *one, it's a limo – there is plenty of freaking room — and two, you're a GHOST! And three, purlease! So what if I can't do the secret handshake thingy? I bet neither of you could make three packed lunches in ten minutes flat, do the rotas for the restaurant and train the youngest for the Spelling Bee, all at the same time.*

Where are we going, anyway? says H.P.H. *This doesn't look like Boston to me.*

After thirty minutes in the car, I have still not managed to get a straight answer as to why the plan has now changed. It doesn't matter how I phrase the question; he manages to avoid a straight answer.

"Linus," I ask, yet again, "why is THE MOST FAMOUS RAPPER IN THE WORLD in Worcester? Why is he not in Boston?"

"Man, he just likes to mix things up," Linus says, not looking up from his phone.

"But I thought he had a gig in Boston tonight?" I persist. "I thought that's why we were recording IN BOSTON?"

Linus leans forward, getting right up to my face. "Like I said," he says with a scowl, "he likes to mix things up."

I decide to leave this alone for a while. Instead, I look at my watch, do a quick time-difference calculation in my head, and scroll down-to find *"Home"* in my speed dial.

"Bloom residence!" trills a voice.

"Beverly! Everything alright?"

"Oh, yes," she says, in her ultra-efficient way. "Chicken

casserole and baked Alaska for dinner. Both children are in bed now. I sewed the button back onto Emily's school coat. I'm just about to make their lunches for tomorrow."

Man, she is a dream.

"Thank you so much; that sounds really great. Can you please remember that Logan needs his football kit for the game on Wednesday or Thursday? I think he might need new shorts; I left a note. And Emily really needs to practice vocab for her French test. I left little sticky notes all over her room with the translations, so she sees them all the time. She's getting so much better, but I really don't want her to lose confidence after she got ten out of ten last time. And I think we need to start thinking about the next time Zack comes home; he mentioned he was bringing friends... Anyway, give them a big kiss from me."

"Of course," the Wonder Nanny says. "Don't worry, Stephanie, I already sorted the football shorts and Emily practised her French after dinner. It's all under control. Just concentrate on your work there."

Some people think that the baby and toddler years are the hardest but, when it comes to parenting, the challenges just evolve; different ages, different issues.

I remember walking with Beverly to collect Emily from school, the day before I was leaving to go on a tour in the U.S., for the release of "Bombshell". It was just a few months after she'd started working for us. Emily was struggling at school with her English and math, and Beverly suggested we get her tested for dyslexia. It turned out that Emily *was* dyslexic. But, with hard work and determination, in addition to working her butt off all year, she ended up winning the award for Sustained Effort in Academics, at the school's annual prize-giving.

Beverly also helped to deal with issues Logan was having with some of the boys in his class. Beverly just talked it through with me. She told me how her own son, now a dental surgeon, had been bullied when he was Logan's age, and how her other son had also struggled with his spelling. I had a ton of rehearsals and media interviews that week, and H.P.H. was away on business so, between Beverly's on-the-ball presence and Bubby flying back and forth to give them grandma cuddles, I felt like the kids had support.

"I know how to deal with this, Stephanie," she said; "I'll be there for Emily and Logan. Don't neglect your work – *please.* Just remember what a positive message your work sends to your daughter. It's important at her age to see that women can achieve amazing things as well as being great mothers."

She just made me feel calm. She was right, too: I shouldn't feel guilty about loving my work. It didn't mean I loved my kids any less.

"And how is the incredible recording session going?" Wonder Nanny asks, her voice trilling as she finishes her sentence.

"Well, we are getting there – put it that way," I say. Which is entirely truthful, until the limo starts slowing down, then comes to a complete halt.

I take the phone from my ear. "What's going on?"

Linus shrugs. "Man, I dunno. Traffic?" We both look out of the window. The other lanes of traffic are flowing freely. Nope, we have pulled over to the right. Shit. This is not traffic; this is a full-on breakdown.

"Bev, I gotta go!"

The car is still for a few moments, before the driver knocks on the window and tells us to get out. He doesn't know what the problem is; something about the engine overheating. It won't go and he thinks it's unsafe to stay inside.

What?! We need to sit by the side of the road and wait for the breakdown truck to arrive?

"Did you bring a coat?" I ask Candice. As usual, she is dressed like she's going to a club. Which I suppose she is, in a way. But she is *definitely* not dressed to leave a club and walk home in minus-three degrees.

"Err, I packed a coat. It's, like, somewhere in the bag." Giving me a look which says, *"Come on!"*, Candice says: "Did you?"

To be fair, I am wearing a leather jacket, but it is not the kind that does up and, frankly it's not really going to do my body temperature much good in this weather. And I'm totally *NOT* putting on a hat; I just had a very expensive blow-dry before we left! Yet another thing that went on the emergency Amex card.

Outside, the grey skies stretch for what seems like forever. It's almost dark. I start to shiver the moment we step out of the limo. It is cold. Bone-chillingly cold. Linus fishes out a packet of cigarettes from his sleek, white bomber jacket and offers me one. I'm not a regular smoker, but I do enjoy an occasional sneaky cig. *Oh, go on, then.* I lean forward as he gives me a light.

"Thanks."

"No problem, man."

We stand in silence as the traffic streams past, the limo's hazard lights pulsing in the gloom. My mind flits back to Bazza's tweets about how I've dissed the scene that made me, and I feel sad and a bit lost. The truth is, I guess I am. A widow, the heir of a failed family business, standing in the cold, on the edge of a highway in the middle of nowhere, chasing an elusive dream…

The phone goes again.

"Mrs. Bloom? This is Rose Green from the *Evening Standard*."

"Yes?"

"Do you have any comment on the closure and sale of the

Café Michael restaurants founded by your late husband?"

What?! How the heck did she get my number?

"Er, no, no, no comment," I say in shock, and immediately put down the phone. I'm already cold, but I go even colder as the realization hits: it's out there. There's no hiding it now. It's now just a matter of time before everyone – the staff, the kids, the P.T.A., the employees – finds out that the Café Michael chain is a busted flush. Also, I just basically told a journalist to piss off. First rule of being a pop star in your forties: *always* be nice to journalists.

"Hey," says Candice, tapping me on the arm, "I think someone is coming to save us!" She points off into the distance, and I see the orange, flashing light of a pickup truck approaching us through the gloom.

When it pulls to a stop, there is some chatter between the limo driver and the breakdown guy, followed by some intensive shrugging of shoulders. Then, I watch as the guy from the breakdown truck places a hook on the front of the limo. The car judders as it's hoisted onto the back of the breakdown truck.

"They're taking the frickin' limo? WHAT THE…?" I start jumping up and down. "Are you kidding me?!!"

Linus comes over to me. "Hey, lady, don't sweat it." He flashes me his iPhone, showing an app with a map and a pin which is flashing, slowly moving across it. "We already took the bags out and Uber's three minutes away, man."

When our new ride – a beat-up, navy Honda Civic – arrives, Linus helps the driver stuff the bags into the tiny trunk. Not all of the luggage fits, and our carry-ons are now stacked on the front seat. The three of us squeeze into the back of the car and sit in silence for the duration of the ride. Barry Manilow's "I Write the Songs" blares on the radio. Ironic.

"Oh, my god, I am so happy to see you!!!" I yell at Beaver when we arrive in Worcester. He is waiting on the steps of the hotel, as we all spill out of the car and scramble up the stairs.

"I wouldn't go in there, Steph, if I were you," he says, shaking his head slowly.

"What d'ya mean?"

Beaver sucks air through his teeth. "Did you see the text from Alejandro?"

I look at my phone. Alejandro has indeed sent me a WhatsApp, about an hour ago: "Just to warn you, love, Beaver says hotel equals total slum."

"Oh, come on," I say, "it can't be that bad!"

"Okay, well, that…" he says, pointing to the door of the 1960s-style, flat-roofed building, the Worcester College Campus Inn, "…without being too rude, is the Hotel Du Fucking Slum."

Okay, so, Ale was being accurate. I look at the door. I can

see that about one-and-a-half of the three stars which had once been etched onto the glass door have actually been scratched off. I look at my make-up artist. He looks at me and purses his lips, as if to say: "Told you so."

Beaver has been at my side doing my make-up for years now, and his over-exuberance makes me smile. His über-campness makes him seem the ultimate stereotypical gay but, to be honest, there's nothing stereotypical about him.

Although, there was that time when I was with Beaver in Paris. Zack texted to tell me that Drogba, the football striker, was returning to Chelsea after playing for another team, and Beaver mistook *"Drogba from Chelsea"* for a *"drug bust"* on *"Made in Chelsea"*, the U.K. reality-T.V. show. When I said we were talking about the Chelsea footballer Didier Drogba, Beaver replied: "Girl, I do *Dancing on Ice*; I do *not* do football!"

Or, the time he used some gay hook-up app and a super-hot guy replied to his message. Beaver was so excited when the doorbell rang, he answered the door wearing nothing but his favourite leather thong and matching beret, only to find that the man on the other side of the door was his porter bringing him an Amazon package.

"Okay…" I say, struggling to find the positives, "so, it's not the Lenox. But, c'mon, Beavey, it's THE MOST FAMOUS RAPPER IN THE WORLD!" My palms are outstretched. "I'd record in a freaking public toilet for him!"

Beaver smiles broadly, convinced. "O.M.G., O.M.G., O.M.G.! Steph, can you even BELIEVE it?! We're here! You're recording with THE MOST FAMOUS RAPPER IN THE WORLD!" He puts both hands in front of his mouth and does a little Edvard Munch-style scream, then jumps up and down and gives me the most ginormous bear hug, lifting me off the ground. "*Arrrgggggghhhhhh!*" I almost forget about the shit hitting the fan in London.

"I know, I know – I'm so excited!" I say, when I'm back on the ground. "I can't believe this is actually happening. How was your pit stop in New York?" I ask. "I saw you were at the Mercer, hobnobbing with some seriously hot guys!"

"Yeah, it was crazy, babe!" says Beaver, hands on hips. "I flew to New York straight from the Coconut gig. Got to Heathrow by the skin of my teeth, and actually made it to the Michael Kors after-party in Manhattan last night, before coming out here this morning!" Beaver takes a deep breath, then adds: "I am literally running on espresso and five-hour energy shots!"

Linus lumbers up the steps past us, carrying the bags. "Hey, man, I thought you hated the cold," he says to me, holding open the door. "Come on in."

He's damn *right* I hate the cold. The ONE thing I don't miss about my hometown in Canada.

"But I'll tell you this, Steph," Beaver says, as we walk in: "I already downloaded the Lenox menu. I really wanted the yellowtail sashimi and one of their award-winning espresso martinis... And what do we get instead? Hotel de Fucking California!"

"Oh, stop kvetching," I say.

Candice screws up her face. "Huh? But we're not in California," she says. "I thought that was why I needed to bring a coat."

Inside, it's like the millennium never happened. Or the Millennium Bug was actually real, and time never moved on. Most U.S. colleges have an on-campus hotel – you know, the kind of place where you put up your parents and your bubby when graduation time rolls around. Let's be clear: they are not five-star places. They do not have Thalasso spas and fancy boutiques selling Cartier and Prada. . . nor do they have Michelin-starred sushi restaurants. They are not those kinds of places. They are the kind of places with ugly-patterned carpets, bad strip-lighting and the type of furniture you'd find in an early-1990s, made-for-T.V. movie. They have vending machines in the corridors selling chips, twinkies and high-sugar drinks. Thinking about it, they probably don't have professional recording studios which, therefore, do not make them the kind of place where you'd want to record a track with an international superstar.

I make this point to Linus, who is leaning against the reception desk sorting out a bunch of room keys. He seems unperturbed.

"So you know," I say, waving my hands around, trying to make myself as clear as possible, "all this really isn't what I was expecting."

Linus does not reply, instead handing me a room key. "Bar's over there," he says, nodding to his right. "Dump your bags. We'll see you there."

"Sure," I say. It *really* was not a question.

We head upstairs. Oy vey, what a tatty lift. Whenever there's a lift in my life, there's usually a problem. There was the time when Logan got stuck between two floors in a lift in a hotel, during a holiday to Florida, and the fire service had to come and rescue him. And then I got stuck in a lift in another hotel, during a romantic mini-break with H.P.H., except I was only wearing a bathrobe, as I was heading back to the room from the spa. And, when the firefighters came that time and prised open the door, I had to slide panty-less through the crack in the doors, and jump down into the arms of a hot fireman, who could surely see up my dressing gown. Thankfully, H.P.H. was playing golf.

Ping! Third floor. I peer out of the lift and follow the signs to room #328.

There's always a moment of excitement when you open the door to a good hotel room. I remember when we visited the New York Café Michael, just after opening the one in London – a triumphant homecoming. We stayed at an incredible suite at The Mark on the Upper East Side, and H.P.H. carried me through the door with a rose in his teeth, throwing me onto the huge bed, with its crisp, white linen and fur throw. I remember the deep, rolltop bath, a huge bowl of fresh fruits and an ice bucket with a bottle of Veuve Clicquot. God, I miss that. I miss him.

Gingerly, I open the door.

Cream and red bed linen? Mahogany veneer?

I take a peek in the bathroom. Old bath. *Plastic* shower curtain?! Is that mould around the taps? I go back out and poke around in the mini-bar: instant coffee and freeze-dried milk? Certainly a dive. Won't be Instagramming this for Wachman and the other P.T.A. moms to see. I haven't stayed in a place like this since the first time Tony booked me into one of my first gigs, in Blackpool.

I collapse onto the bed, flop back against the pillows and flick on the cable, half-watching an infomercial for an electric potato peeler. Do those things even work? Looks ridiculous but, at $39.99, an absolute bargain. Even comes with one of those spiralizer thingies for zucchini. Maybe I'll get one for Beverly.

It's not long before there's a knock at the door. My heart pounds with excitement. *EEK! This is it! It's Linus, to tell me THE MOST FAMOUS RAPPER IN THE WORLD is here!*

Nope: Beaver.

"Hey, Steph, is your room as bad as mine?" He pushes past me and inspects my bathroom. "Yep, I thought as much —

although, I think your shower curtain might have slightly more mould. We can swap if you like," he says.

Beaver sees my face fall.

"Hey, don't sweat it." he smiles. "I *loved* 1991. So chic."

Beaver and I go downstairs, as instructed. Candice says she's not feeling great and is going to take a nap. Sure. No doubt the combo of being up late the night before, plus the jetlag, has thrown her.

As we stand in the elevator, I keep looking at my phone. I'm expecting it to start blowing up any moment, with *"What's going on?"* messages from the P.T.A., or calls from the kids, but it hasn't. Maybe the story hasn't been published yet. Maybe they can't do anything without my comment. Maybe it's been published, but is so uninteresting that it's been buried halfway down the page and no one has seen it. The adult in me knows that's total B.S.

It really is only a matter of time.

Chapter 5

"Meet Da Crew"

Linus is in the bar, surrounded by a group of men with huge roadie boxes and bags. He gestures to us to come over.

"Hey, man, lemme introduce you to da crew."

Linus goes around the semi-circle of very large guys in hoodies and designer jeans, drinking bottles of beer, Coke and what looks like whisky on ice. "Star Roberts, meet Jello K, L-Frenzy, aka. Def Swagg, EmCee Sean M, D.J. Taxi and, finally, the one and only Z-Drive!! We have pretty much known each other all our lives."

"Hi!" I say, flashing them a Star Roberts megawatt smile. "I am *SO* excited to meet you all! And so pumped to be recording with THE MOST FAMOUS RAPPER IN THE WORLD. Psyched! He'll be here soon, right?"

I'm trying *really* hard not to sound desperate, but a small part of me feels slightly out of place.

The guys all slowly nod at me. Several times. Linus says: "Chill, man."

"Not very conversational, are they?" Beaver whispers in my ear. He orders two Cosmopolitans, despite the fact that I probably shouldn't be drinking, and we stand there like a couple of uncool white kids at a gangsta rapper convention: Eminem Soccer Mom with her Fairy Gaymother.

"So, er, been to Worcester before?" I say, turning to Z-Drive, who seems to be the youngest and friendliest member of the rappers' posse.

"Nah, man, but it cool," says Z-Drive. "We go where he goes."

"Of course, of course you do." I take a gulp of my icy-cold, pink drink. "My P.A. does the same," I say.

He shakes his head. "I ain't no 'personal assistant', lady," he says, using his fingers as air quotes.

This is like being at the worst P.T.A. meeting *ever.*

"So, how do you become a member of THE MOST FAMOUS RAPPER IN THE WORLD'S POSSE? Did you, like, apply?" I say.

"Man, how I got here? I dunno," he grins, "quite a story." His expression suggests there is much more to Z-Drive than meets the eye – perhaps more than he's prepared to tell.

But I battle on: "So, did you, like, apply?" I'm now talking fast and flapping my arms about. "Was there, like, an advertisement? I bet there was a ton of competition. My son Logan applied to do an internship in a software company last summer and, let me tell you, with all those other Chelsea kids... it was *tough.*"

"Man, it don't matter," says Z-Drive, "it ain't that interesting. But you, lady, I reckon *you* are. Not many grown-up mommas starting out in da biz, ya dig? So, how the fuck did a lady like you get here?"

The truth is, I never set out to be big in dance music; I always wanted to be a singer, ever since I was a little girl singing Yiddish songs to the old Jewish bubbies in the local nursing home. But, as I matured, I was always more of a rock chick than a dance music diva. The 1980s were my era. Big hair. Big shoulder pads. Big, black leather jacket. Def Leppard, Mötley Crüe... I worshipped their sound. The first band I joined, when I was fifteen, was called Hot Back. We wrote and played original hard rock, as well as the requisite heavy-metal covers, gigging in bars and clubs all over Ontario. I dreamt of becoming like Ann Wilson of Heart. When I graduated from high school, my band and I were booked to go on tour – an unbelievably HUGE thing for a kid. But my folks weren't having it.

"You on the road with four guys? No way!" my mother said. My father – as he always did – agreed with my mom. No, no, I was not for the road; I was to get into a great program at university. And so, being a good Jewish kid, I went off to study, instead. When I told my band I wasn't going, they were seriously pissed but they still went on tour; they just hired a new singer. My lesson: almost anyone is disposable in showbusiness.

So, how did I get here?

"Well, I guess it all started that night in Notting Hill," I say to Z-Drive, as I recall the charity gig in London, the night I realized that my life was going to change. It was a one-off concert to promote the record I'd made with a youth charity organization, and it was a huge deal for me.

"One of the cover tracks of the charity album was remixed by a young D.J. affiliated with the charity, and the song started shooting up the dance charts. I was touring small-time clubs and pubs across the country, trying to make a name for myself as a recording artist, but this Notting Hill concert was huge; it was the first time I performed in London after my husband died. All of my friends were there, including Alejandro and Giovanna, of course. Plus, Zach, Logan, Emily, my mother and even my brother flew over from Ottawa; everyone I cared about was there supporting me. The kids in the charity, who sang and played on my record, were loving their moment in the spotlight, and I was in my happy place: on stage again."

"Sounds sick, man," says Z-Drive, after listening to the condensed version of my climb up the rickety ladder of "fame".

"Anyway," I continue, "after the concert, we go home. It's past midnight and everyone in the house is down for the count. Then, suddenly, I'm awakened by the sound of booming dance music; I'm like: *What the hell is that?*' The music is so loud, like it would be in a club. At first, I think it's my kids, Zack or Logan, playing a prank on me, and I think that everyone is going to wake up! I fumble around, turn on the bedside lamp and realize it's coming from the speakers on the bedroom T.V. But the T.V. itself was off, weirdly; it was just the sound that was blasting. I find the remote and, after a couple of fumbles, turn it off. The music was insanely loud and there's no way everyone slept through it. And, yet, the house is completely still. I creep upstairs to where the kids are sleeping – silence, only broken by the occasional and unmistakable snore of my brother, who's crashing at my place. They're all still asleep? Seriously? How can they not have been awakened by such loud music? And, not only that, how did that music come on?"

Z-Drive's eyes are now as wide as saucers. "So, what was all that noise? Friggin' robbers, looking to steal your shit?" he says, listening intently.

"Well, no, actually," I tell him. I pause and look around me, realizing that I now have the attention of everyone in the posse. "There was no one there. So, I creep back to my bedroom, get back under the covers and fall asleep almost immediately. And then I have the *most* vivid dream.

"It really *was* a *seriously* strange dream! I was in a restaurant, which was all made out of glass. I could see the maître d' behind her podium; two men were standing behind her, both of whom I recognized: my husband and my father. Now, you understand, I know that both of these guys are dead, my father for about three years, and my husband was killed a year or so before this show.

So, you know, I'm naturally excited to see them. I rush into the restaurant to greet them: 'K.C.! Daddy!' My father waves at me and continues chatting with the maître d', as if everything is perfectly normal. And, when I reach them, H.P.H. leans forward, smiles and touches my neck, and says: 'Hi, Dolly,' just like he always did. And then he tells me: 'This is YOUR time. Now is YOUR time. Music is your dream and you have to do this.' The whole experience was so real, I could actually feel H.P.H. touch my neck and it startled me awake.

"At this point," I say, as I subconsciously touch the back of my neck while recalling the dream, "I'm really freaking out, and I phone Alejandro, my best friend, who is half asleep but listens to the story, and wakes up enough to argue that there must be a rational explanation. 'Steph,' he says, 'I get it; you've got a lot going on. You've finally released a record. This is a *big* deal for you, and your husband and dad aren't here to see it. I'm not surprised you're dreaming about either of them. The music? Tch, it was just some freak electrical fault. Seriously, just a coincidence.'"

"Yeah, I could be down with that explanation, man," nods Z-Drive.

"Yeah, I guess," I say to the group. "But I couldn't let it go. I decided I'm going to turn on the T.V., just to see if it had been left on a dance music channel; maybe something just turned it on. But, when I turn on the T.V., it's not on any channel; I have to scroll through the menus to get to M.T.V. And, what's on? A T.V. show called *Daddy's Girl*. *Daddy's Girl?!* I've never heard of that show! And, in the early hours of the morning? *I* was always 'Daddy's Girl'! It was just too weird. Then... there's a knock at my door..."

"Oh, my god! Who is it?" Jello K gasps. "Fuckin' robbers, right? The feds?"

"Nope, my MOTHER! And she's freaking out, too! And she says: 'Steph, someone just came into my room! They turned on the light. Then they turned off the light and shut the door. Was it you?' So, I told her what had just happened with the music, the T.V. and the dream. Mom nodded. 'Daddy and K.C. were here,' she said. 'They were both here in this house.'

"A few days later, some dance music producers contacted me. They've heard 'Band of Gold' and thought we should collaborate. We wrote the whole album in the end, co-writing a bunch of other dance tracks. And then everything goes insane: I'm playing festivals, sports events, Gay Prides and gigs all over Europe; I'm on stage in Miami, Vegas and L.A. And then THE MOST FAMOUS RAPPER IN THE WORLD hears a song I wrote about the dream I just told you, sends someone to see me in a club in London, and tells my manager he wants to write the rap for it. So, that's how I got here. That's how a Chelsea Soccer Mom ended up in Worcester Massachusetts, with THE MOST FAMOUS RAPPER IN THE WORLD."

"Whoa! That's some really cool shit, man," says Z-Drive, shaking his head. "Lady, we need to chow. Let's get somethin' to eat."

In the restaurant, we all squeeze around a large, round table in the corner of the room.

Somehow feeling more like I really do "belong" there now, I decide this is the perfect opportunity to give Linus the "secret handshake" that he showed me in the car. I splay out my palm and he smoothly slides his hand over mine, but I clumsily forget to flip it to the other side, and end up fist-bumping the inside of his opened hand. Linus shakes his head. "Nah, bro, you still ain't got it."

I throw my head back in laughter. Then I start to feel my phone buzzing continuously in my pocket.

From Franz, written in separate, line-by-line text boxes:

"Stephanie, I don't like to text."

"But an article has just been published."

"In the Evening Standard about Café Michael closing."

"We need to reconsider the formal announcement of sale."

"I will forward the link."

And from Tony:

"How's the Lenox, babe?"

The Lenox? I question, as I read his message. Linus had said he told Tony we were moving from Boston to Worcester... *didn't he?!*

From Candice:

"Just gonna pop down to the 7-11 and eat in the room, babe."

From Zack:

"Film crew on their way, Mom. To Worcester, as requested. I know you don't like me to swear, but seriously? Worcester? WTAF. xx"

From Emily:

"Logan's acting weird, Mom. When are you coming home?"

Not sure which one to answer first.

The server is moving around the table, taking our orders. Everyone is getting burgers.

"What can I get for you?" she asks me, pen poised over her notepad.

What a question.

I order a salad. I am barely five feet tall (and that's AFTER a Pilates class!), so, for as long as I can remember, I have always watched my weight. I can go up and down a dress size if I gain or lose just two kilos. My daughter says that, when she gets older, she wants to be as glamorous as me, but DEFINITELY taller! Even though I consistently tell her that "good things come in small packages", she hopes that she is not as vertically challenged as I am. But only time will tell whose height gene she inherited.

When the food arrives, the guys fall over the plates like they've not seen food in days. But not before Linus brings out a small bottle of red sauce. He takes the bun off his burger and drips a few drops onto the meat patty, then replaces the bun top and passes it around the table. Each member of the posse does exactly the same: bun off, few drops on the burger, replace bun. It's a small bottle, a bit like the ones they put Tabasco in, but this one has no label.

"What the hell is that?" I say, thinking I'm making some kind of joke. "Some kind of secret sauce?"

Silence.

I toy with my salad as I watch them eat. The speed with which these guys are necking back the protein is insane. I'm not sure anything could distract them from their reverence of the great American burger and fries.

Nothing apart from their phones, of course – the largest, most blinged up and current of iPhones, which they sling down onto the table as they eat. It reminds me of those old Wild West films, when an outlaw struts into a saloon and slings his gun down on the bar.

Oy vey, I really shouldn't have watched that darn movie on the plane last night.

I watch the posse laugh and joke, as they dip fistfuls of fries into ketchup and slug back beer. Although I feel like I've just connected in some way with the crew, I slide a bit closer to Beaver.

"You alright, babe?" he asks, perhaps sensing a little fear.

"Yeah, sure," I say brightly, before some lines from a rap start to flit through my head: something about motherfuckers and guns. Oy vey.

"Hey, man, don't fucking steal my fries!" Z-Drive snaps suddenly, as he swipes D.J. Taxi's arm out of the way.

"I ain't stealing your fries," says D.J. Taxi. "Shut the fuck up, man, else we'll take this outside."

We are not in Chelsea anymore, Toto.

Suddenly, all the phones start to flash and vibrate. Linus is the first to pick up. He studies the screen, shows it to Jello K, then they both get up and leave. EmCee Sean is next. Again, he studies the screen, shows it to D.J. Taxi, who then picks up his phone and looks at the message. I'm straining to try and see what is happening on their screens. I have no idea what the heck is going on but, one by one, each member of THE MOST FAMOUS RAPPER IN THE WORLD's posse picks up his phone, stands up and tears ass out of the restaurant.

"Did that just happen?" says Beaver, looking around at the half-eaten burger meals on the table.

"They didn't say goodbye, right?"

About a minute later, we start to hear sirens. Sirens and sirens and sirens. Tonnes of them. Getting louder and louder and louder. I'm tempted to run to the window, to see what's going on, but worry that would just look like I was scared. I don't want to admit that I am.

"Do you think they're coming here?" says Beaver.

"I'm sure it's just some kind of accident… probably downtown," I say, trying to sound calm.

The sirens fade away. Silence.

"Shall I text Candice, to see if she wants to come down?" I say.

"Sure."

Candice is always almost surgically attached to her phone, but there is no answer and the text remains unread. Beaver says he'll go and check on her.

I sit alone for what feels like ages, toying with the rest of my salad and doom-scrolling through my phone, before I sense someone standing beside me. I look up. A tall, gawky, twenty-something guy in a red, goose-down parka is beside me.

"Er, Mrs. Bloom… um… Stepha—I mean, Star? Hi," the kid finally blurts out. "We're Zack's friends. You know, the film crew?" He extends his hand to shake mine. He says his name is Josh and he's the director, before introducing his friends, Tom (camera) and Sam (sound).

"Oh, yes, yes, great! So pleased to meet you," I say, still distracted by the en masse disappearing act. "Thank you so much for coming."

"Yeah, no problem. Jeez, it's cold out there," Josh continues. "And cops literally EVERYWHERE! So, yeah, anyway, can't wait to get started." I don't think he draws breath. "So, where's THE MOST FAMOUS RAPPER IN THE WORLD?"

"Um, he's not here yet," I say.

"Oh. Well, I'm starving; those burgers look great. Do you know if they've got bacon in them?"

"ARRRGGGGGHHHHHHHHHHHH!!!"

Beaver is back in the restaurant, red-faced, panicked and screaming.

"Candice is not in her room! She's gone!" he yells.

Then the hotel front door swings open and three cops walk into the building.

Chapter 6

"I'm Your P.A., So Let's P.A.... R.T.Y!"

We've been looking for Candice for almost two hours, but she's disappeared. She's not in the 7-11, where she said she was going to buy something to eat; neither is she in any one of the three student bars, the two Starbucks and an all-night diner, which I am sure I saw Logan watching on *Diners, Drive-Ins and Dives* a few weeks back.

But at least she's not in the Worcester General Hospital emergency room; I phoned there already. It's as though Candice has literally vanished into thin air. It is dark and bone-chillingly cold, and, complicating our search, much of the downtown area is locked down.

"Do you remember when Candice bought those fidget spinners for Hanukkah, because she couldn't find Dreidels?" I say, to no one in particular.

"Huh?" says Beaver. "Do you think she fell in the river? Maybe she got run over?" he says, panicking. "Do we need to check the hospital again?"

I keep checking my phone, to see if she's picked up her messages. I don't understand it. Candice is permanently attached to her freakin' phone! Has she lost it? Maybe it's in a gutter. Is SHE in a gutter? Is she being held hostage by some kind of terrorist, or... or, worse, a gunman?

I keep thinking back to the cops in the hotel. We watched them as they started talking to the woman on the front desk. The cops then started pointing at the restaurant before heading toward us. They walked right around the restaurant, nodding at us as they passed the booth.

I shifted into cliché mode as I asked: "Everything alright, officer?"

"Just checking things out," he said. "There's been a disturbance locally."

Before I could ask what happened, he walked away.

Josh taps me on the shoulder. "So, er, Steph, I love what you did back there; it looked great. But maybe you could just enter that bar again and turn to the camera, this time a bit longer, so we can see how concerned you are?"

I forgot that the film crew is with us, too. Josh, the director, said that of course they could help us look for Candice, and anyway, great T.V. is all about the drama. Well, one thing is for damn sure: there is way too much drama around here right now.

"Josh, love," I say, "you are here to make a promo video; you are *not* Michael freaking Moore. And, at the moment, you're meant to be helping us find my missing assistant. I *am* concerned. I do *not* need to do this again for the camera so I look more… Freakin'. Concerned."

"Sorry," Josh says, and embarrassment spreads over his face. "Erm," he says, staring at his feet, a student once more. "Where do you want to look next?"

I look down the main street and gesture that we move toward a sea of flashing blue lights. As we move closer to the taped-off area, the extent of the local disturbance becomes clear. People are everywhere. Cops are standing guard with guns; investigators taking statements from bystanders; forensics officers in white suits going in and out of tents, photographing evidence. The police tape makes it instantly clear that there's been some kind of shooting. And this is no T.V. cop drama or *Fox News* report. It is sobering. This is the reality of gun crime in America, and I realize that, living in Europe for over a decade, it's something I haven't had to think about for a long time.

"There! There she is! Candice! Candice!" Beaver yells. He grabs my arm and points maniacally across the street, at a female figure who is being led out of a bar by a couple of police officers. Her head is bowed, but I can see the woman has long, dark hair and is wearing an unmistakable, pink, faux-fur coat. She is also in handcuffs.

Oh my god! He's right: it's her!

"Candice! Candice!" I scream. "Are you okay?"

I don't think she can hear me. She is now being helped into the back of a police car. People in the crowd all around us are getting out their phones, and taking pictures and videos of the scene. I crane my neck, straining to see more as I lean into the crime-scene tape, pushing it out of the way.

"Candice? Candice?!!" I yell again, like a crazy woman. "Are you okay?!"

A police baton presses up against my chest – hard!

"Hey!" I yell, reaching out to protect myself from the baton. "I need to get my assistant!"

"I'm afraid you can't go any further down there, ma'am," an officer says, firmly. "Ladies and gentlemen, you need to move back, please."

For a split second, I consider going against his wishes, then I see the anger in his face. So, I switch gears, grab Beaver's arm and pull him back with me, through the crowd of people obsessed with filming every single second of this drama. We are both now in tears, watching as the police car drives away with my Candice in it.

Worcester police station is even more of a dive than the hotel. Battered walls, rusty chairs, dirty floors, bad strip lighting… it makes the hotel look like the freakin' Ritz.

I walk up to the reception and ask the officer behind the desk: "Can you tell me about the girl you just brought in?"

"Girl?" The officer rolls her eyes.

"Well, woman," I correct myself. "Young woman, early twenties, pink fur coat – fake fur! Just want to point that out! I think it's my assistant. She's been missing now for at least four hours and I can't contact her on her phone. I'm really worried about her."

The officer rolls her eyes again. "Does your assistant have a name?"

"Candice. Candice Porter," I say.

Beaver is grasping onto my arm, supportively. "Yes, yes, Candice Porter," Beaver repeats, in a very clear and highly-articulated British accent. "Long, dark hair, always has IMPECCABLE eyeliner – which, I must tell you, is a very hard thing to achieve."

The officer glares at us like we are from the outer reaches of the universe. "Right, Candice Porter – I'll check that name for you, ma'am."

"Thank you," I say, just as my phone starts buzzing in my pocket. *Candice? Oh, please, God, let it be Candice.* I dart to the corner of the room, barely registering the screen before I answer.

"Hello?"

"Hello, darling…" says a quiet voice at the other end line.

"Mom? Are you okay? It's kinda late."

"Er, well…" My mother's voice trails off, in a way only she can manage.

"What's going on, Mom? Shouldn't you be in bed?"

"Well, yes, I suppose I should, darling. What time is it?"

"Mom, have you been drinking? Is everything okay? What's going on?"

She starts to sob.

"What? What?! I'm in a police station!" I hiss into the phone, my hand cupped over the microphone.

"It's Gerald," says my mother, between sobs; "he's... he's... had a heart attack. On the boat. At the captain's table. Black-tie dinner."

A heart attack?! The words make my head spin. I am immediately transported back to my father's death. That dreadful call in the middle of the night. H.P.H. holding me while I sobbed on the edge of the bed. A heart attack. *The* heart attack that killed my daddy.

Okay, Steph, breathe, breathe... I shake myself to calm down.

"Mom, Mom, stay calm, please. Is he okay?"

"I... don't know," my mother stutters.

I cannot believe I am hearing this. If Gerald dies, it will catapult my mother back into grief.

"He just looked so pale, Stephanie! At first, I thought it was perhaps that his shirt or bow tie was too tight. Or maybe that he was choking on the smoked salmon blinis. But no, darling, he just collapsed! Right there! Then they took him away on a stretcher. With an oxygen mask! Stephanie, what am I going to do if he dies?!"

I bury my head in my hands. This is why my mother shouldn't be allowed to date. She was crushed by my father's death, despite his health issues having put so much strain on her for so many years. Despite us knowing that his kidneys were failing, and that he probably wouldn't be around for that much longer. Despite all that, his death still came as a massive blow.

"We were having such a lovely time, too," my mother sniffs. "He lost his wife a few years ago, you know? Gerald... well, I think he just wanted someone to share some good times with. He really takes care of me..."

It's funny that she said that, because it's always been the other way around: my mother has always taken care of other people. She loves to; it's in her nature. But maybe she has always been meant to find someone, after my father, who wants to take care of *her*. And, even though I have yet to meet Gerald, I realize that my mother must really care for this guy, and a part of me really hopes this isn't a short-lived episode in her life.

I've often thought that people's paths are pretty much set. The eerily cross-eyed medium I saw at the Spiritual Society of Belgravia, before my music career really took off, said so, too. "You have free will, dear one," he told me, "but there are some things that *will* happen – *do* happen – for a reason."

Actually, Tony said the same thing when I first got hot on the dance scene, and I kept banging on about how all I really wanted to be was a rock chick. Granted, that was after quite a few G-

and-Ts at Annabel's. Anyway, the point is, maybe Gerald was always going to turn up for my mom after my father died. Maybe this was always going to happen, in a weird, synchronistic, planet-aligning sort of way.

"Anyway, darling," my mother says, composing herself, "I'm going to the sick bay now. I think we'll need to come home to you. Do you mind? I'll call you when I know more."

"O.M.G., Steph, have you seen this?" Beaver is suddenly waving his own phone in my face.

I snap back into reality and pull my head back, so I can get a look at the screen. "Stop moving it about, Beaver! I can't see it properly."

Then, "Who is *that*?" I say, pointing at a picture of the back of a short, blonde woman, who looks to be in an argument with a police officer.

"That's you, like, literally minutes ago, in the street, having a barney with the police before we came here," Beaver says, breathlessly. "Except now it's not on the streets; now it's trending on SOCIAL!"

"Where?"

"Twitter, Instagram, Tiktok, SnapChat and Facebook." He makes a little *"shit,-I-did-try-and-warn-you-this-was-bad"* face.

Sure enough, it's all there. Originated on Twitter, from the @Barryspeaks account, in a particularly snarky tone.

"Looks like @StarRoberts, who has turned her back on her TRUE

fans, is already in trouble Stateside." The hashtags *"#recordingwithrappers, #noloyalty, #crime, #police, #trouble, #StarRoberts"* are in bold under the picture.

I have no idea how it got taken, nor how Barry got hold of it, but none of that matters; just like the restaurant shit, it's out there now. And it will spread. It'll only be a matter of time before my kids, my friends, the P.T.A. moms and my fans see it, too.

"Ma'am? Ma'am?" a voice is calling me from across the room. I look up from the phone and see the officer behind the reception desk beckoning to me.

"Your assistant," the officer says, "Candice Porter? We have no one here under that name, ma'am."

Is this a reason to feel relieved or not?

"Since it's only been four hours, I can't list her as a missing person yet, ma'am. But I'll get the ball rolling, just in case she still doesn't turn up by tomorrow afternoon," the officer says, twiddling her pen over a form.

"Tomorrow?" I say, feeling sick. "Yes, please, we should probably get the ball rolling, since we're already here."

In the cab back to the hotel, I stare out of the window, as the lights of downtown merge into the semi-darkness of the university campus. Beaver is leaning against me in a drink-induced sleep.

I squeeze his arm reassuringly, then turn back to my phone and click the link to the newspaper article Franz has sent me. It's only short, but it's damning enough.

"CAFE MICHAEL TO SHUTS ITS ICONIC DOORS
By Rose Green, Chief Business Reporter.

"Cafe Michael, the Chelsea restaurant loved by the rich and famous, is set to close after the business failed to gain back losses sustained during the pandemic.

"The restaurant on the King's Road will likely close at the end of the month, as will its New York City counterpart of the same name. It is believed that neither eatery managed to gain back enough losses sustained after closures due to the pandemic, despite a wholesale renovation at the London restaurant, which is thought to have cost the company hundreds of thousands of pounds. A source said the closures will see many job losses.

"The restaurant, famous for its Italian take on modern cuisine and stellar wine cellar, opened ten years ago, and has welcomed countless celebrities through its doors.

"Stephanie Bloom, widow of K.C. Bloom, who died three years ago, remains the chairman of the restaurants. She was not available for comment when contacted by reporters. Ms. Bloom, 43, is also known by her stage name Star Roberts, has carved out a career as a minor dance-music artist since the death of her husband. She is *currently believed to be in the United States recording a new single.*

"K.C. Bloom, a long-time entrepreneur and widely regarded as a hugely talented restaurateur, was tragically ki—"

I'm not reading any more. A freaking *"minor dance-music artist"*? I slam the phone into my lap. I'm furious.

The P.T.A. moms have obviously read the article, too, because a message I put on the fundraiser WhatsApp group is immediately read and goes unanswered.

And still no Candice. I look at the last text I sent her: status still unread. Various catastrophic scenarios run on a loop in my head.

And then I decide I'll check my emails again. Maybe Candice has sent a message and it's gotten into my spam folder? I mean, she *does* sometimes write almost *entirely* in emojis. Like those books you used to read as a kid, where pictures replaced letters or syllables and you had to guess the word or phrase... except with emojis it's way more complicated. For example, Candice once told me that a red heart sent on WhatsApp means: *"I want to sleep with you"*, but if you post it on Instagram it means *"f**k off"*. Not sure I believe that, but speaking emoji is way more complicated than the Yiddish I learned growing up.

I scroll through my spam folder. Okay. Russian lovers in my area; Viagra ads; badly-executed scams; weird things which are mainly symbols and don't make any sense; all shaken and stirred with the usual pervy fan mail, which Candice mostly manages to isolate into the junk mail. Huh. I used to read it in the early days, when the first record went crazy on the charts. But, after a while, it got worse and worse, so I had Candice scan my inbox for it and block the email addresses.

There's quite a lot here. I really do love my fans, and I am pretty good at engaging with them on social media, but I seem to have collected *quite* a few weirdos, too. Most of the names I've seen before; a couple are new. I decide to open one of them:

"SUBJECT: MILF ASS.
"Whoa, baby, you are a freaking MILF. Next time you're in my hood I'll be there waiting for you. I'm gunna take yo MILFY ASS 4 cocktails. I'm gunna show you good time, fo sho."

I knew there was a reason I didn't read those emails. I close it down as quickly as can, feeling slightly dirty. As I said, most of my fans are super lovely, but there are some of them, unfortunately, that are just perverts.

I continue scanning down the junk mailbox. Something… anything… from Candice? One of Candice's many friends? No, nothing.

Then Logan's name jumps out at me, in the subject line of an email. It's from the school.

"LOGAN – URGENT MATTER.

"Dear Mrs. Bloom,

"I do hope you are well. Unfortunately, I am having to write to you about your son, Logan. As you may know, he has been doing exceptionally well in this term's entrepreneurial venture, which challenged students to create a project for the new digital age. Logan designed a 'nano-chip', which could be attached to extremely small personal items, such as earrings or rings, in case they go missing or get stolen. This was a well-designed invention, according to the school's head of technology, who graded it as an A*.

"However, it has since come to our attention that Logan took his entrepreneurial activities one step further and not only produced said chip, but took the product to market, with the support of some teaching assistants and members of the kitchen staff (with whom I am dealing separately, as this is against school regulations). Whilst the product has sold well, it has come to our attention that some of those purchasing the chip have been using it for purposes other than Logan's stated aim, which was to 'help my mother find the expensive jewellery she is always losing'. Indeed, we have discovered that Logan's chip has controversially been used in tracking members of the school, and some parents have raised concerns around data protection.

"The school cares very much about creating and nurturing the entrepreneurs of the future, and as such we do not wish to punish Logan for this. However, we cannot condone a business that supports hidden surveillance of any kind.

"In this case, we have ruled that your son is benched from all A-Team football matches until further notice.

"If you would like to discuss this matter further, then please do not hesitate to contact me.

"Yours faithfully,

"Mrs. Belinda Smart, OBE, M.A. OXON

"Headteacher.

"The Church of England Boys' and Girls' School of West London

"Motto: 'Contendunt facti sunt numulariis, advocatorum vel doctoribus redditur.'"

Oh, my god – my kid is a frickin' genius! Are they bloody serious? I really *do* need one of those nano-thingies! Insurance companies would go bonkers for this sort of thing! And yet, the school is punishing him? Kicking him off the football team?

Staring at the letterhead of The Church of England Boys' and Girls' School of West London, I think back to the process of finding schools for my two boys, when we first moved to London. Schlepping around prep schools in the rain for my then three-year-old son, who was, at that time, very happy in his *very* Jewish Manhattan nursery school, was tough. I looked at all sorts of places, with old-fashioned uniforms and school chapels, and wondered how I would deal with transitioning my son from playing a talking potato latke in the Hanukkah recital to starring in the nativity play, as one of the wise men coming to worship the new-born Jesus Christ.

It's so easy being Jewish in New York; New York is a *very* Jewish city. They close schools on the Jewish New Year and even suspend parking restrictions so that you can get to synagogue. But, in Britain, where there's no separation of church and state, while there are still pockets of Jewishness, it's not like it was in New York. For one thing, they certainly don't suspend the parking regulations in Kensington and Chelsea on the Jewish New Year, and I got the parking tickets to prove it.

After a few weeks in rainy London, I remember thinking that we would get used to the English way: "Rule Britannia" and all that. And we *did*. We chose a school that the royals go to.

Still, while I am kinda secretly impressed with my son's business prowess, he has been selling surveillance chips and I am going to have to talk to him. And this is not the time for text talk over WhatsApp…

"Hello…" a dozy, teenage voice answers.

"LO-GAN?!!!"

"Waaaah? What? Mom?" Logan says. "What's going on?"

"LOGAN! Wake up!" I scream.

"Okay, okay, Mom," he drawls. "Jeez, I'm awake, I'm awake. It's, like, four a.m."

"You know what?" I say, crossly. "I don't care what time it is in London."

There is a rustling of bedsheets.

"Logan, am I hearing this right? You created a chip which can be used to secretly track people???!! Mrs. Smart has just emailed me. Logan, are you insane? Surveillance?? YOU ARE SIXTEEN YEARS OLD!"

There is a moment's silence, as my teen son doubtless computes the extent of the trouble he may be in. Then, the inevitable diatribe begins:

"Yeah, Mom, I *did* take the business live and, by the way, it's doing GREAT. But, those chips, they aren't for tracking PEOPLE; they're for tracking small *things*, like diamond earrings. I know how mad Dad used to get when you were always misplacing your jewellery. I was inspired to create something for you, Mom! It's not meant for people to spy on other people! Anyway, it's *reeeeallly* not fair. Now I'm off the football team and that numbnut Lucas Wachman took my place as midfielder! I can't believe it!"

What? The Wachman kid took his place on the team? And a midfielder? Seriously? That kid can't even play. He struggled to make the C-Team last semester.

"Mom. Mom! Are you listening to me?! I mean, I can kinda see how it might have happened... but I *SWEAR* I didn't even know. It was just a dumb chip for finding earrings... I had no idea what people were using it for!"

"Honey," I tell Logan, "it's okay. We'll sort out your place on the team, okay? And, just so you know, your invention is pretty cool. Maybe think next time about the full consequences of how these things can be used, though, eh?"

There is another moment's silence, before Logan says: "Okay, thanks, Mom." Then: "Mom, I was just trying to make some money – for us, you know? Now that Dad isn't here anymore. You don't have to be the only one trying to make ends meet. I was just trying to help out. And especially now that the restaurants have to shut down."

What the...?!

"You know about the restaurants?"

"Of course I know, Mom," says Logan. "We *all* know. Constanza overheard Alejandro talking about it at home, and she told Emily. But everyone knows, anyway; it's in the newspaper."

"Oh, Logan," I say, feeling tears pricking in my eyes, and this enormous pang of guilt that I wasn't there to tell or reassure them in person. They don't deserve this crisis – not after losing their dad. "I'm so sorry you guys had to find out this way. But don't worry, hun. I didn't think I had to tell you because we're going to be... just fine." I punctuate the words as my heart sinks down to my toes. "Save me a couple of those incredible nano-chip-thingies, 'kay? And don't worry about your place on the team; we'll sort that out."

"Sure," says Logan, his tone immediately more relaxed. "Emily said you'd say that. She says we should just concentrate on being kids, doing well at school, and feel secure in the knowledge that you are Mom AND Dad now."

Emily said *that?*

"Anyway, how is it going with the rapper, Mom? I told everyone at school that you were going to be a worldwide star."

Oh, God. I decide on a quick change of subject: "Is everything else going okay?"

"Oh, yeah, Mom, everything else is great. Beverly made some great Russian chicken thing last night, before she went out. With this potato, too, with cream and cheese. Totally yummy."

Beverly left the kids?

"How long was she gone?"

"Not long, maybe a half hour," says Logan, yawning. "I taught Emily how to do a Rubik's cube. "Can I go back to sleep now?"

"Okay, honey," I say. "As long as you're okay. And don't worry; it's all going to be fine."

Beaver, who has been leaning into me and fast asleep for the whole journey, now flops his head onto my shoulder, which wakes him up.

"Did Candice call?" he says, as he bolts upright.

"No, darling, not yet," I say.

"She's going to be okay, right?" Beaver says, needily.

And I say the only thing I can say: "Of course she will, my love."

Chapter 7

"Thou Shalt Not Mix Whisky and Weed"

It's almost midnight when we get back to the hotel. The place is still buzzing: students milling around the bar, drinking shots and bottles of beer, arms around each other, hugging, singing, chatting and cheering – making up for lost time. But there is no sign of the rapper's posse and still no sign of Candice. As we head for the lift, Beaver is silent. I rub his arm, attempting to try and reassure him.

"The police will let us know if there is something. I don't think we can do any more tonight. We just have to wait."

"Yeah, I know," Beaver says sadly, as we walk down the corridor. "Come on, I'll walk you to your room. Like a proper gentleman."

We walk on down the corridor, and I root around in my purse for my room key, taking longer than usual because I feel so drained. And then my phone rings.

It's my mother. She's breathless and panicked. "Darling!"

"Mom! Are you okay? Is everything alright?" I ask, fearing the response.

"Well, no, actually. Gerald only had a mild heart attack and we're at the airport now, flying to London," she says through her wheezes. "They've managed to stabilize him but he'll need a stent. We're rushing for the gate now. I'm trying to keep up with the air hostess pushing him in the wheelchair. She's very speedy!"

"He had a heart attack and you're going to London?"

"Yes, dear. London. Gerald's best friend is a cardiac surgeon in Harley Street; he wanted him to do the stent. I called already and asked Beverly to prepare the spare room for us. Hope you don't mind."

With everything else that's going on? *Oy, oy oy…!*

"No, of course I don't mind, Mom."

"Thank you, darling."

Click. She's gone.

Beaver is rolling his eyes at me, and I'm about to start explaining when I hear a clunking noise down the corridor. I look up just in time to see a couple of pairs of legs disappear into a room down the hall. Not Candice's legs, though, and not Candice's room.

"Why's everyone up so late?" I say out loud, half to Beaver, half to myself. "Don't any of you want to sleep?"

"Man, it ain't so late; still time for a drink," says a male voice, and I see a face pop out behind a door. It's Linus. Then another face pops around the door: Z-Drive. They both smile and Linus gestures for me to head over.

For a second I smile, but almost immediately anxiety rises up inside me and I find myself literally pelting down the hallway, only just managing to stop myself flying straight into his room.

"Hey! Hey!" I scream. "Where the hell did you all go?!"

Linus puts his arm across the door, closing it behind him and Z-Drive.

"Hey, man," Linus says, quietly, "calm the heck down!"

"WHERE'S CANDICE?" I freak out. "Where the hell is she?! And, again, where the hell have you all been? What happened at dinner?"

"Hey, man, calm down. We just went out," Z-Drive says, holding his hands up in a surrender pose. "Candice? What?"

I must have raised my voice a little too much, because a few other doors have now opened; people are poking their heads out, trying to see what's going on.

"Sorry, everyone," I say to the hallway, crisscrossing my hands in a bid to show everyone I didn't mean to make a scene. "Misunderstanding."

My half-assed apology is met with a muffled chorus of "fuck you" and "keep the noise down". Beaver is now behind me, hand on my arm, trying to calm me down. It's not working.

"You need to tell me where you went! I'm still waiting to record the track!" I hiss, not quite believing my courage in leaning right into Linus's face – well, his chest, because he is so darn tall. It does nothing.

"Hey, Mrs. Star, I don't need to tell you shit," Linus says, dangerously. Then, almost instantly, his face suddenly breaks into a broad smile, as if this is all some big old joke. He opens the door wide. "But you are both still welcome to come in for a drink... aren't they, Z?"

I look at Beaver. Should we? I'm still slightly apprehensive. He shrugs, a hint of mischief in his smile. *Oh, okay. Hell, why not?*

I sit cross-legged on the couch in the corner of the room; Beaver perches on the arm next to me. Z-Drive wanders over to the desk and grabs a bottle of Courvoisier. He opens it, grabs a few glasses from the bathroom and pours each of us a large measure. I stare at the dark liquid and make a mental note to sip, not gulp.

"Ladies first," Z-Drive says, handing a glass to me, then one to Linus. "Cheers, man."

"Well, cheers," says Linus, downing the entire glass in one. Beaver does the same. Z-Drive immediately refills it.

"Cheers," I say, taking a little more than a sip. Jeez, this stuff is strong.

We sit in silence for a few seconds and I look around the room. Two double beds; Z Drive and Linus are obviously sharing. Couple of laptops; a few shirts and jackets over the back of the chair at the desk. Surprisingly neat for two guys. Oh, and the whole place smells heavily of weed. I'm not sure what to say and, because I'm starting to feel ever so slightly nervous, I neck back the rest of the glass. My throat burns.

"So, what's going on, man?" Linus says, slumping back onto one of the beds. "You been out enjoying Worcester?"

"Well, I wouldn't say 'enjoying'; we've been looking for Candice," I say, nodding at Beaver.

"Hey, man, don't worry about your assistant; she'll come back. She's probably at some club with the college kids; forgot to take her phone or no signal. It's all cool."

How can she be at a club when the whole town is locked down after a shooting?

"Well, it doesn't feel 'cool' to me," I say, sounding way more Nagging Jewish Mom than Cognac-Drinking Pop Star. "She's barely twenty-five, and somewhere in the middle of Massa-frickin'-chusetts! I wanna know where she is! What if something horrible has happened to her?"

"Man, seriously, just relax," says Z-Drive, knocking back a load more cognac. He opens a packet of chips and pauses before leaning forward, resting his elbows on his knees. "You know, I had this time when my girlfriend went missing; I was just left at home, thinking she was dead or something. She didn't come home for two days. Two days! I was going insane. Turns out she had to go look after her grandma, who had fallen down in the kitchen at home. She was at the hospital and she didn't have any time to take much with her, and her phone just ran out of battery. I was so pissed at her when she came back, but she was just focused on making sure that her grandmother was okay in the hospital, and she didn't think about me. And, you know what that taught me, man?"

"Er, what?" I say.

Another swig of cognac. "Well, a couple of things, actually."

"Go on..."

"One: patience, man – it's a virtue. And, two: the worst, man – it rarely fuckin' happens."

"That's the thing, though," I sigh: "sometimes the worst really *does* happen."

I can feel alcohol already in my bloodstream: that point where you think, *Oh, wow, this is nice; I'm quite chilled out.* My shoulders sag and I realize how stressed I am. I take another great big gulp and it all just comes out: "In fact, sometimes it's the very, *very* worst thing that happens, and it happens when everything else is going SO WELL."

Linus and Z-Drive lean forward, listening intently.

"And that thing is... a helicopter which crashes in some canyon outside Los Angeles and kills your husband."

There's silence for another moment, then Z-Drive says, animated: "Man, I think I remember that crash. The one in Bell Canyon, a few years back? Big fireball? Came crashing down in a gorge? *Ka-boom!* Was all over the news. Couple of bigshot businessmen onboard – both killed. Shitty."

Linus kicks him. "Shut up, man."

"It's okay," I say. "Yes, that's the one. My husband was out in L.A., scouting for a West Coast location for our restaurant. You may have heard of Café Michael?"

"Yea, best steak in New York! Whoa, dat's *your* place?!" Z-Drive asks.

Linus rolls his eyes at me. "Sorry," he mouths, "he's just a kid."

I go on: "Well, it was really my husband's dream. We opened one in London and K.C. – that's my husband... I mean, my late husband – thought it was time to widen the Café Michael brand, and he started the process of branching out into luxury boutique hotels – you know, high-end rooms, spa, gym. And, of course, the Café Michael restaurants and signature steaks. That kind of thing."

I was getting quite animated now, as I remembered my husband's passion for the project, how much he wanted to expand, and how pleased he was that the London restaurant was doing so well. How life was just going to get "better and better and better..."

"Anyway," I smile, for the first time warming a little to Linus, "as you say, it was a remote canyon, way up in the hills outside L.A. Incredible views; amazing hiking and biking trails. The perfect spot for a luxury weekend retreat. There was going to be an infinity pool which had the most spectacular views. There was even this cliff-side area where he was told we could grow our own grapes, to make our own wine. K.C. had all the plans and the permissions in place. All the investment was secured. It was a done deal. Anyway, that day he went up to the site with the architect; he messaged me that morning and sent me a few pictures of the canyon: there was magnolia in full blossom, and a picture of the tree trunk where he carved our initials. He wrote: *'I can't wait to show you this, honey, xoxo.'* It was the last message I ever got from him. On the way back to L.A., the helicopter's engine cut out; just stopped, suddenly. A total freak. A one-in-ten-million fault in some tiny part of the engine, the investigators said…"

Silence descends on the room. Then I hear Beaver, who is now curled up in a ball at the end of the sofa, sniffling, tears streaming down his face.

"Sorry, Steph, I just remember what it was like for you and the kids," he says, wiping his eyes. "I honestly don't know how you got through it."

The cognac in my system is powerful enough to dampen my latent grief, but I decide to spare the guys the story of the aftermath: the fateful call at one a.m. from an L.A.P.D. cop; the shock and doubling over in bed, crying uncontrollably – crying, crying, crying… streams of tears turned into oceans. Trying to imagine my life now without My Rock, the Love of my Life. Trying to figure out how to tell my kids their dad was actually gone. And then, once they knew, how would they react? The funeral, the shiva, time off school, going back to school, therapy sessions... My mom even moved in with us for a while. But there wasn't a night, for the better part of a year, when I didn't have at least one kid sleeping with me in my bed.

But this time I don't cry. I smile weakly at Z-Drive who, momentarily, looks uncomfortable amid my story and Beaver's sniffling, and fiddles with his glass, turning it and tipping it, focusing on the liquid as it moves around.

Then, as if by magic, Linus's phone starts buzzing. He looks pained and points to the screen helplessly, as if to say, "Babe, I have no choice," then goes into the bathroom to take the call.

I used to do that a lot, didn't I? K.C. says in my head, and I smile, thinking of all those times he'd get up from a dinner table mid-meal, or leave movie theatres, shows and parties to take "important business calls", at all hours of the day. I strain to hear what Linus is saying, or if I can hear what's being said at the other end. Is it the rapper calling? Is he coming? Who knows? All I hear is: "Yeah, okay, okay. Uh-huh. Yeah, sure."

Then Z-Drive suddenly comes out with: "Wow, that's rough. I'm sorry, man."

"It's okay, honey," I say, as I look at him and suddenly realize that he's just a kid himself. He can't be more than twenty-three or twenty-four – as old as Candice. I feel a sharp pang, remembering that she is still missing.

Z-Drive continues: "So, the restaurants... I guess the L.A.

place never got built? But at least the London and New York ones are still there – and you, man, must have inherited the whole thing, then? When your husband died?"

"I, er…"

"She lost her *husband*, man. Her kids lost their dad!" Linus is back from his phone call in the bathroom, and is glaring at his young roadie.

"It's okay," I say to Linus. "Yes, well, I did inherit the whole business. Except now that's gone, too." I take another big gulp of the Courvoisier, then hold out my glass to Z-Drive, who immediately refills it and also pours more for Beaver.

"Thanks," we say in unison.

"What do you mean, gone?"

"I mean *gone*. Finished. Done. Closing." I stick my head in my hands. "We just never made it out of the pandemic: too many losses. Not that I knew how bad it was, of course; I mean, there were still plans to expand! I sure as hell wouldn't have just spent gazillions on a revamp at the London place if I'd known."

"That's rough, man." Z-Drive slowly shakes his head.

"Yeah," I say, "especially if it closes forever. I mean, they're both for sale, but it's gone for me, gone for K.C. – though he's dead, so what does he care?" Christ, I'm drunk. "So, hopefully, someone will buy it."

Silence.

"Anyway…" I take a deep breath, "I have my kids. And my

music. That keeps me going."

Linus says: "Yeah, I really feel that." He looks at me again, a sudden understanding in his eyes, and I know that he suddenly sees how important this trip is to me.

I'm distracted by my phone, which lights up with a notification:

"Christina W (Admin) added you to 'New Fundraiser' group."

New? Don't we have enough fundraiser WhatsApp groups already?

I swipe and read the first and only message:

"Ladies, I've set up this group as, with so little time to go, I really think we need to consider alternative arrangements to Café Michael, with all the 'trouble' (*gritted teeth emoji*). CW X."

Then, suddenly:

"Christina W (Admin) removed you from the 'New Fundraiser' group."

The message disappears.

"More drink, yo?" Z-Drive is opening another bottle of Courvoisier.

We've got through the first bottle already?

"Sure, why not?" I say, before suddenly realizing I'm busting for a pee. I start to get up. "Two secs, though; I just need to go to the bathroom."

As soon as I start to walk, I realize that the room is spinning. No, no, it'll be fine. I totter gingerly on my heels. "Whooooa!" I say, falling into the side of the couch, and almost into Linus, who holds out his arms to steady me. I collapse into giggles.

"Hey, man, you okay?"

"Yeah, yeah, fine," I laugh, and feel myself flushing bright red. "I just need to get to the bathroom." Man, I'm so drunk right now.

As I reach the bathroom, my phone buzzes.

"Seen this?"

Alejandro has sent a bunch of screenshots: messages from Christina's *"New Fundraiser"* WhatsApp group. Holding the phone, I rest my elbows on the sink and scan-read it. The thread starts off pretty vanilla, with plenty of helpful suggestions for other venues: the French bistro in Sloane Square; Amanda May is suggesting the big Chinese place off the King's Road; maybe even the school hall. Then Christina says that if all else fails they are "more than welcome" to have it at her house. Her wonderfully huge house. Oy, she always has to have the solution. Then it starts to get bitchy: *"I never really loved Café Michael,"* says one. *"No, and did the new revamp really add anything?"* agrees another. My music is also discussed *("Just too out there, ladies, isn't it?"),* my gigs at The Pink Coconut *("Why? I just ask myself why she bothers…. Wasn't there a ton of life insurance…?")* and my trip to the States. They even laugh about Logan, and the nano-tracker invention which got him kicked off the football team; Wachman has posted a football and a crying emoji. *"Maybe his stalker tracker will help him find a new team?! (winking face.)"* How do they know how much life insurance there was? How dare they suggest my music isn't worth anything? I'm incandescent.

"How did you get this?" I type, furiously.

Alejandro comes straight back:

"Not sure how it got to me, hun. Came from a number I didn't recognize. But it sure looks like one of them wants you to know about it."

Booming rap music starts up outside the bathroom. The room is spinning slightly less now and, after I've peed, I grab a glass and fill it with water from the faucet, downing it quickly, then repeating twice. I look at myself in the mirror. I will not let those mothers win.

"You want a pretzel?" Linus says, as I return to the room and collapse onto the couch once more. I notice that Beaver has fallen asleep, still curled up in a little ball. He gestures to the open packet on the table and sits back in his chair, where he lights up a joint, takes a huge drag and passes it to Linus. I scoop a handful of pretzel thins into my palm, before I cast my eyes up at the smoke alarms.

"Hey, man," Linus says, "chill; we already took out the batteries."

Linus and Z-Drive pass the joint back and forth a couple of times, nodding their heads to the beat of the music. I decline each time they offer it to me. Then Linus presses it into my hand.

"C'mon, chill, man. You need to C.T.F.O., as they say."

Hun, don't you think you've had enough for one day? says H.P.H. in my head. *I don't mean to sound like an "alta kakker",* he says in Yiddish, for my benefit (and, as if anyone can actually hear him), *but mixing the alcohol AND weed will put you over the edge! Stay on point, Steph! Don't you remember the time we went to Jo Jo's in New York, and we polished off a bottle-and-a-half of wine AFTER we had cocktails at the bar first? You were taking your clothes off in the elevator on the way back up to our apartment, and I had to literally hold you up – but I needed two hands to unlock the door, so I had to let go of you and you fell flat on your ass in the corridor. I even took that Polaroid shot of you lying there, hahahaha.*

Oh, purlease! I am so much more adult than that now, I reply, silently.

"Star, you okay, girl?" says Linus, and I realize I am still staring at the fire alarm in the ceiling.

"Oh, yea, just kinda stressed out," I admit. "But, nah, I'm good with the cognac." I hand him back the spliff.

"Yeah, man, you got a LOT on your plate wit the restaurants," says Linus.

"Yeah, well, it's not just that."

Linus cocks his head and gives me what Emily would call a "come on, then, fess up" look. So, I find the texts Alejandro has sent me and throw the phone at them. "Read those," I say, as I hand my entire London social life, exploding on a WhatsApp message, to a relative stranger. I explain about the fundraiser and how it was going to be at Café Michael, and how now they want to change the venue, which only makes the situation worse.

"Oh, come on, man," Linus says, "haven't you got bigger fish to fry? Are you really going to let those mommas piss you off?"

"Well, no, obviously not," I say, although I realize I'd probably be a helluva lot angrier if I wasn't full of cognac. Feeling bold, I say: "Babe, I flew all the way over here to record with THE MOST FAMOUS RAPPER IN THE WORLD, and he kinda hasn't turned up yet!"

"He'll be here, yo."

"Yes, but when?" I ask, sounding ever so slightly stressed again. "I kinda have to get back, and now with Candice missing..."

"Just chill, man. Just chill. Have another drink."

I shake my head. "I really got to get some sleep."

I gently use my nails to tickle Beaver's arm, to awaken him, and he bolts straight up. "C'mon, hun, it's time to get back to our rooms," I say.

Beaver and I are literally holding each other up while we walk down the corridor. He goes straight to his room and, when I reach mine, I collapse straight into my bed and stare at the ceiling. The room has started spinning again, as I curl up under the lumpy duvet and close my eyes.

"You always come up with the goods, dolly," my husband says to me in my dream that night. *"I have faith in you. You'll work it out."*

Chapter 8

"It's a sMall World"

O.M.G., I'm totally, completely, utterly hungover! It's just after nine a.m. and I'm staring at the hotel breakfast buffet. I'm not sure if I want fluffy American pancakes or the greasy French toast, or whether they both just make me want to puke – something which, frankly, I have already done once this morning.

"Coffee?" says a waitress, hovering above me with a large glass pot.

I offer up my cup and smile weakly: "Thanks." My head is banging. I *have* to find some headache pills as a matter of urgency.

"Do you have any fresh fruit?" I ask the server, averting my gaze from the smorgasbord of saturated fat making my stomach churn.

"Fruit salad over there," says the waitress, pointing to a bowl of gloopy-looking, syrupy canned fruit at the end of the table. To be honest, it looks worse to me than the other stuff and I decide to stick to coffee.

I need to check in with the police about Candice. They said they would call if and when they find out anything, but I will feel better if I check anyway. At least I know she probably wasn't one of the victims of last night's shooting; the police have confirmed on Twitter that the two victims were both male. But maybe I should go back through the town, and check some of the bars and cafés again? I try phoning Candice again, for the umpteenth time, in hopes that she will pick up this time around. When it rings through to her voicemail, I toy with calling the police station, even though I know it's still too early for her to be tagged a "missing person".

Linus, in his baseball cap and satiny, white bomber jacket, wanders into the breakfast room. He attacks the buffet with gusto, grabbing a huge bagel and several pieces of bacon, before scooping a huge dollop of cream cheese onto his plate. He slides into the booth and places his plate on the table, nods at me and smiles, then starts to eat, silently.

Josh, my student film director, arrives shortly afterwards, carrying a mug of tea and a plate stacked high with pancakes, fruit and maple syrup. Linus nods at us both, takes another massive bite of his bagel, and chews purposefully before he speaks.

"So, I was thinking," he says, wiping some cream cheese from his chin, "y'all wanna go to the mall today?"

"I'm sorry?" I say, rubbing my head. "Hey, Josh, do you have any Advil?"

Josh – his mouth full of pancake – shakes his head. I text Beaver to bring some when he comes down; he's always got painkillers on him.

Linus – realizing we have not accepted his offer – repeats it. "Yeah, I was thinking we could check out the mall today?"

Seriously? My P.A. is still missing, I'm completely hungover, I still haven't recorded *one note* with THE MOST FAMOUS RAPPER IN THE WORLD, and Linus thinks I want to go SHOPPING?!

Of course, I do not say this.

"Er, really? Shouldn't I stay here, so I'm ready to record when THE MOST FAMOUS RAPPER IN THE WORLD arrives?"

"Not today, man," Linus says, shaking his head. "He ain't gonna make it today."

I feel my eyes close. *Are. You. Fuckin'. Kidding. Me?*

Calm it, Steph, calm it, I hear H.P.H. say in my head.

"Oh, dear, Linus," I say, finally. "That's a shame."

Linus shrugs.

Josh decides now is a good time to enter the conversation. "Er... we could always get some B-roll," he says. "You know, the mall would be a great location to do some lifestyle sort of filming. Always seems to work on *The Kardashians.*"

"You watch that show?"

"Sure," says Josh, utterly serious. "Everyone's watched that show at some point, haven't they? Plus, as a media and film major, it's a must-see. Frankly, that family is a huge postmodern reference for... well, so many things."

Linus takes yet another bite of his bagel and wipes another glob of cream cheese from his chin. He looks at me again, raises his shoulders up around his chin and holds out his palms, as if he's offering me a million bucks and I've told him: "Gee, no, thanks."

"Look, why don't you come and find something to take home for your kids?"

Then Josh chips in: "Actually, I'm just looking now, and the Worcester Mall has some of the most incredible water fountains. I gotta say, Steph, it would look GREAT on camera..." He flashes his phone at me to show me. Hmm, and palm trees, too. They do look kinda impressive.

Beaver arrives at our table with a plate of scrambled eggs. No toast; Beaver doesn't do carbs. He fishes a strip of painkillers out of his pocket. "Here you go, hun. They worked for me." He sees my pained expression. "You okay?"

"They want me to go to the mall," I say, popping out a couple of the pills and necking them back with a glass of water. "Rapper's a no-show again," I say, under my breath.

Beaver has a forkful of scrambled eggs and ponders. "Well, you know, I can always stay here and wait for Candice. Maybe a bit of schpatzing in *Victoria's Secret* would do you some good? We had a seriously rough night; a trip to the mall might be just what you need to clear your head. Go on, Doll, have a good time. Here..." he says, fishing out a lip gloss from his pocket and handing it to me, smiling. "For touch-ups. Don't worry, I'll call you if anything happens."

Linus arranges for a limo to pick us up. I'm not sure whether it's the same limo that broke down on the way to the hotel, but, whatever – it's a shiny, black limo and it looks the part; it definitely says "pop star".

It doesn't take long to get there and, when we do, I realize that I've been living in London for so long I'd forgotten how seriously big U.S. malls are. Like, *crazy* huge! Worcester is a city of, maybe, less than 200,000 people, and this place feels bigger than the town itself. There are neon signs, advertising screens and escalators everywhere, and stores from Target to Victoria's Secret, to J.Crew and Gap. In the distance, there's a cavernous food court with everything from McDonald's and California Pizza Kitchen to Sushi-in-a-Box, Wings 'n' Things and Ben & Jerry's. The people milling around look like little consumer ants.

"So, I think I'm going over here, man," Linus says, pointing at a sign which says: *"Food Court"*. He waves his gold iPhone above his head as if it were a trophy, as he walks off. "Text if you need me, bro." Food Court? We've only just had breakfast! Hey, I'm not going to argue.

Sam, Josh and I look at each other, as if we're kids who've just been dumped somewhere totally random by Mom and Dad, and we're not sure how far we're allowed to stray.

"So… what do you guys want to do?" I say, still a little

perplexed as to why we are here.

"How about we get some B-roll?" says Josh. "Maybe we could follow Star Roberts as she goes shopping?"

Okay, let's do this. I spin around, checking out the nearest shops. How about a new bag? Nope, can't see a bag shop; we'll have to do that later. Kids' clothes? Too busy; full of strollers. Hmm, where else?

Josh points to an upscale male boutique: Luxury by Larry. "How about here?"

I feel a pang. H.P.H. used to get all his suits custom-made in Italy or on Savile Row, but whenever I went away on tour I always used to get him a new tie – blue with dots, usually. That was our deal. H.P.H. had a classic style when it came to formal clothes, and stuck to it. I smile to myself as I remember how getting a tie for him was sometimes easier than at other times, because I played some seriously dive-type places in the beginning – way worse than The Pink Coconut. Let's just say that gas stations on the M1 are not the best places to find great male attire. Jan would disagree, of course; his idea of smart clothing is a tie with naked girls on it.

Inside the shop, piped opera music is playing low, and instinctively I head over to the ties, running my hand over the selection laid out: orange with green stripes… Paisley pattern… weird, flowery thing… I pick up a navy silk with red dots. *That's the one I'd choose,* I think. "Gosh, there are some lovely ones here,"

I say out loud, internally wishing I still had someone to buy for.

"Oh, there really are, aren't there?" a waspish voice from beside me sighs. "And the suits, too. You'd think with a choice like that he would be able to just pick one and get on with it. But apparently not." I look up and see a tall man in his mid-forties, leaning against the display. He is staring toward the entrance to the fitting room.

"Stan? Stan? Are you done in there yet?" he hisses, exasperated. "We REALLY need to get on with this."

"Oh, dear. Having one of those days?" I offer up. "I have two sons myself, and let me tell you—"

The man looks at me. "Fiancé," he corrects me, "not my son. He's my fiancé. He's picking out a suit for our wedding. Well, trying to, at least."

"Oh! Congratulations. Mazal tov!" I say, instinctively. "Marriage, eh? Well, that is a whole new world of compromise."

"Oh, I think I'm already finding that one out," the man says. "This is, like, the seventh store we've been to already – and I cannot stand shopping."

"Well, I guess those are the things you do when you love someone," I say.

"Oh, yes, of course," the man smiles. "He wants the perfect suit and I want him to have what he wants. So, that's how it goes. Just like he wanted a job in Boston, and we left our life in California so we could be together. It's all love and commitment."

It makes me think about all the huge compromises that both H.P.H. and I made over the years for each other, and for our family. Much more than dragging him out to go shopping when he didn't want to. *Much* more. I look again at the guy who's waiting for his fiancé to come out of the changing room, and think to myself that going shopping when he doesn't want to probably won't be the biggest compromise he has to make in future.

A man emerges out of the changing room in a particularly smart Tom Ford tux. He's looking straight at me.

Mr. Exasperated says: "Stan, that looks SENSATIONAL! Now, let's buy it and get the hell out of here."

But Stan is not listening. He's staring straight at me. "O.M.G., are you Star Roberts???" he says.

"Erm… er…"

"O.M.G., you ARE! Harry, Harry, look who it is: it's STAR ROBERTS!!! I read that she was in the States this week!" The guy in the tux flings himself at me, engulfing me in a bear hug. "Hi! I'm Stan and this is my fiancé, Harry. Do you know, I just love you! Don't worry, I'm totally vaccinated. We all are, right?"

He turns to his fiancé. "Harry, do you remember when we were in Manchester and we saw Star at Pride, then again at The Pink Coconut, when we were in London? Do you remember that night? *'I Am a Woman and I Know What I Want, Ya'!*" he sings, and grinds vigorously.

The salesman looks shocked. I expect he's worrying this guy might split the Tom Ford tux. And I totally get it; Tom Ford is freaking expensive.

"O.M.G.," Harry continues, "I just loved that song. We're having that on our wedding playlist. Maybe not the first dance, though; that's Mariah Carey."

"Oh," I say, "that's great. And when are you getting married?"

"April, in Hawaii. Can. Not. Wait! Thought about here, obviously, but Hawaii is so much better weather at that time of year. Just picking out our outfits for the Special Weekend. Oh, my goodness, it's such an honour to meet you! I can't believe it! I mean, I read all the stuff about how you were recording with a big rap star, which is absolutely fine, in my opinion – just so you know – because I know there has been some negativity out there—"

"Well, that's fabulous," I cut him off. "It's always such a great honour to meet my fans."

"Star," Stan leans in, conspiratorially, "I know this is terribly indiscreet, but I just have to ask, because I am absolutely in your corner, aren't I, Harry? Is it true what they're saying about you online? Is that really you in the picture, having an argument with the police?"

I decide to play dumb. "Oh, what picture is that?" I say

sweetly. "I don't think I've seen any pictures of me recently. I've been so busy recording over here..." I fib.

"O.M.G., you haven't seen it? What? It's EVERYWHERE, girl!" Stan is whipping out his phone, and proceeds to show me every single instance of the picture, in every single gossip and gay website I have ever heard of. One of the headlines reads: *"Is this Pop Singer and Recently Failed Restaurateur Star Roberts Taking Her Anger Out On The Cops?"*

The salesman, looking increasingly nervy, approaches. "Sir, did you have any thoughts about that suit you're wearing?" he asks Stan. "It does look particularly splendid."

Stan looks at the sales guy as if he's insane. "Of course we're going to get it. I look incredible! I might even wear it out of the store!"

"Don't do that," says Harry. "I'm not having it cleaned before the big day."

"Star..." Stan is looking sheepish, "can we get a selfie before we go? We're coming to London soon, honeymooning in Europe. Don't suppose we'll get to see you again at The Pink Coconut, though..."

"Sure you can. I play there a lot."

Stan looks at me oddly. "But they're closing. I follow their Facebook page; they announced it last night."

I have no time to react, as my phone starts to buzz.

"iMessage From Beaver:

"I've got Candice! She's fine. Explain later. xxx."

Chapter 9

"Thou Shalt Listen To Your Heart And Eat The Fried Chicken ;)"

O.M.G. He's got Candice! She's okay. O.M.G., thank the Lord! A wave of relief hits me.

"He's got Candice! She's okay!!" I yell.

"O.M.G. Thank goodness she's OK. Is she back at the hotel?" I type back quickly. *"What happened?!"*

The grey speech bubble appears. Then it disappears. Then it appears. And disappears again. Finally, a three-word reply comes through:

"She's absolutely fine. xxx."

"I'm coming back to the hotel right now," I text back. I don't get a reply.

"That's great!" says Josh, his head popping out from behind the viewfinder of the camera.

"What?!" I say, looking up.

"Yeah, really great, Steph: the whole jumping thing; the outpouring of joy after the grief of last night, and the worry about the media getting hold of images of you in trouble with the police. Finally, we're getting PROPER NARRATIVE here. But maybe you could just do it again? Say the same stuff, obviously, but this time jump a bit higher when you punch the air? And maybe hug the other two guys, as well?" Josh gestures to Harry and Stan, who do not need asking twice.

"Group hug!!!" Stan yells, and leaps toward me with such force that I fall into a display mannequin and slap-bang onto the floor, as one of my wedges flings across the room. The mannequin's head falls off and rolls around on the floor.

"Oh, shit, I didn't press the record button!" says Sam. "But that looked amazing. Can you do it again?"

Harry and Stan take about a zillion selfies with me, and get me to sign a bunch of autographs and record video messages for their various friends and family. They're a super-cute couple – chalk and cheese; Harry the more serious, clearly exasperated, but adoring his over-excitable, ebullient fiancé. They are clearly deeply in love and it makes me feel grateful that, through my music, I am a part of this scene. That I've been welcomed into a world I really knew nothing about before my songs were remixed by two dance D.J.s.

It actually makes my stomach churn, and I feel even more upset about the picture of me that Barry tweeted. Apart from the fact that the picture was completely taken out of context, I don't understand his anger. I'm not being disloyal to my fans by recording with a rapper, am I?

And what the hell is going on with The Pink Coconut?

Closing? I text Tony the question.

"Anyway, so lovely to meet you!" says Stan. "We absolutely love you! And don't let the haters get you down, Star. Who says house and gangsta rap don't mix? *He-llo!* I'm so down with that!" he says, while making some sort of rap-star hand sign, which clearly shows that he's never hung out with "the posse" like I have.

Harry and Stan head to the cash register. Harry puts his arm around his fiancé reassuringly as they pay for the Tom Ford suit. I smile, feeling how blessed I am to have had so many good years with my love. H.P.H. and I first got together when we were practically children.

It was Christmas Day. I was just twenty-one. Like every year, my parents and I went to Florida for Christmas vacation. We flew down to Miami from Ottowa, to get some sun, and had been out to eat Chinese food because, well... we're Jewish, and the Chinese restaurants are the only ones open on December 25th. Anyway, after the meal, my parents went back to the hotel and I headed out to a club with my friend, Charlotte. The club was busy, and we were drinking by the bar when an adorable guy in a yellow sweater came up to me and offered to buy me a drink. A few hours later, I phoned my mother and told her I'd met the man I was going to marry.

My mother's response: "You're drunk, Steph. Come home."

I did go back to the hotel where my family was staying, but the next evening future H.P.H. invited me out for dinner. My parents reluctantly let me go. I was twenty-one, for Chrissake, but lemme tell you, they were NOT happy.

"Who is this guy?" they asked. Not from our town; my dad didn't know his third cousin once removed and my mom didn't play bridge with his mom's best friend's sister! As I left the hotel, they followed me down to reception and hid, Scooby Doo-style, behind the Christmas tree in the lobby. My mother had decided she was going to write down the licence-plate number of H.P.H.'s car so they could track me... just in case I didn't come back.

When my father told the story at our wedding, some years later, he said he always felt that two Jews hiding behind a Christmas tree, spying on their future son-in-law, was both odd and extreme... but my mother told him it was all for the greater good: "She's our only daughter... Even that serial killer Ted Bundy was very handsome and charming – and look what he did!!"

"Are you okay, Steph?" Josh says. "You look like you were daydreaming there. Looks fantastic on camera, but just checking you're not about to faint?"

"Yes, all fine," I say, snapping out of my reverie. "C'mon, let's go find Linus and get out of here. I want to go see Candice."

The mall is more crowded now and, as we wind our way toward the food court, people are obviously now looking at us: a petite blonde in a random mall, in a suburb of Massachusetts, with a camera crew in tow.

Wandering, we soon spot Linus, sitting in a corner seat at Elmo's Chicken Shack.

"Hey, Linus! We found Candice," I call over to him and wave. He waves back, beckoning us over to where he's sitting, busily eating chicken and fries, a large cup of Diet Coke by his side.

"Man, I love me some wings with my hot sauce," Linus says, literally licking his lips.

I look at the plastic basket of fried chicken in front of him, and the little bottle of red sauce on the table. It's the same bottle that the crew all passed around the table when they were eating burgers... before the police sirens shrieked and they all disappeared.

Linus sees me looking at the bottle. "MMMM... MMM... so good! You want some?"

I shake my head. "Not into fried chicken – especially this early," I say; "it's barely noon."

"Ah, c'mon," Linus says. "Sit down. Try it."

"Oh, alright." I sit down in the booth next to Linus and, as Josh sets up the camera shot, I pick up a chicken wing and place it on a spare paper plate. Linus proffers me the sauce. I take the bottle and look at it suspiciously. Dark red. No label. I look around at the other tables. Sure enough, Linus is the only one with this kind of bottle. The hot sauce drips all over the table; I catch a whiff in my nose. Wow! It smells really great.

"Is this your sauce? Are you a chef?"

"Ha. No, we developed it with Da Boss," says Linus. "You gotta think outside the box with revenue streams."

"Yeah, like the Kardashians," Josh says, nodding his head.

Gingerly, I open the bottle, not wild about the fact that there is no label. I mean, shouldn't these things be tested?

"Sis, it ain't poison," says Linus, reading my mind.

"Well, you know, just checking…" I say, and sprinkle a few drops onto the chicken wing, before slowly bringing it up to my mouth to taste.

OH. MY. GOD! Wow! It's sweet and salty and spicy, with just the right amount of heat. It's like a symphony on the tongue. Absolute pleasure! I'm not really into overbearing spice, but I do love great flavour, and I've honestly never tasted something so delicious on a chicken wing.

"This is bloody amazing," I say, forgetting I have a mouthful of chicken. "What's in this stuff?!"

"Ah, that's our secret. But, essentially, five types of chilli, garlic, sugar, salt… you know, the usual. But, then…" he says, with a wink, "a hint of something special." He skips a beat. "Good, eh?"

"It's *incredible!*"

"Think we should go into production?"

"Yes!"

"That's what they all say, sis. It's special stuff, the Rapper's Secret Sauce."

I sprinkle some more of the sauce onto what's left of the chicken wing.

"Hey, don't suppose you guys want to buy a restaurant?" I say, half-jokingly.

When Linus doesn't respond, I go bright red and I'm thankful when my phone buzzes. Even if it is Franz.

"Stephanie! I have great news! We've got a buyer! I'll email over all the details."

Oh, no...

"I thought we were going to wait 'til I got back to London to discuss this," I say in a small voice.

"Stephanie, it's a great offer! You won't get another one of these in a hurry; you gotta snap it up. For the good of the company. For the good of your family. For the good of everyone."

I feel a pang in my stomach, then I'm saved by the beep of another incoming call.

"Sorry, Franz," I say. "Yes, send over the details. I need to go.

"Hello?"

"Steph, it's Mom. I need to talk to you for a sec."

"Is everything okay?"

"Yes, the kids are really delish," my mother replies. "Just

having a coffee – decaf for Gerald; we don't want to raise his blood pressure too much."

"No, obviously not. How is he?"

"Fine. His friend scheduled the stent surgery in a couple of days."

"Oh, good. That's a big relief."

There is a pause and then she says: "I'm far more worried about Beverly, if you really want to know."

"Mom, what are you talking about?"

"Well, she's not here, for a start."

"Of course she's there, Mom. You must be mistaken."

"She's not, Stephanie; she's gone out. Again. I've been watching her. She disappears for hours at a time, even when the kids are there."

My mother has lost her mind.

"Mom, you have only been in London a day, at most. And so what if she's going out a bit more? You're there! She knows you always help out with the kids when you're at the house. So, of course she can go out a bit more. You know Beverly would never let us down! C'mon! I bet she asks you first, before she goes out, right?"

"Well, yes, I suppose she did say..." my mother admits, but clearly still not convinced.

"Well, then."

"I saw your P.T.A. friends, as well," she adds. "Sounds like the plans for the fundraiser are coming along well. They seem very excited... Said they can't wait to see you."

"Oh (mental roll of the eyes), I bet they did. Well, that's great, Mom. I gotta go."

My head is now buzzing with frustration.

"Okay," I say to Linus, slipping the phone back into my bag, "can we please go back to the hotel? Candice is there and I need to see her, to make sure she's okay."

"Hey, what's the rush?" says Linus. "Your lady, she's been out all night, eh? She'll probably want some shut-eye before she has to explain herself to you."

"Please, Linus," I say, "we go now, or otherwise you're not getting this back." I pick up the anonymous bottle of secret sauce off the table, and put it in my tote.

Linus gets up from his seat and starts walking away. "Go for it, sis; got plenty more."

"Where are you going now?" I ask. "I need to see Candice!"

Linus says: "I am going to the bathroom. Then, man, I'll call the limo."

The other two disappear, as well, and I'm left at the table alone. I toy with a chicken wing, absent-mindedly dipping it in a pool of the secret hot sauce left on Linus's plate, pulling off the meat with my teeth. God, it really is good. Reminds me of when I was pregnant; each time, with all the kids, all I craved was spicy food. Whatever is in this sauce is pure gold.

Stephanie, did you just eat not one, but three fried chicken wings? says H.P.H. in my head. *That must be one hell of a sauce.*

Buzz, the phone vibrates. Again. Message from Tony:

"Hi, Steph. Yes, such a shame about The Pink Coconut. Sorry you found out like this; they were hoping to keep it quiet. I was going to tell you when you got back."

What?! I'm ringing him now!

"C'mon, c'mon... pick up, pick up!!!!" I hiss into the phone. I've only just managed to get him to accept that it's the 21st century and he needs a smartphone (it was me who took him to the Apple store to get one, actually); I'm pretty sure he can't have already worked out how to put the thing on silent, like the rest of the world. No, that's not him. That's not Tony. So, if he's not picking up, he's either dead or in the loo.

"Hello?" says a voice, finally.

"Tony!"

"Yeah?" He sounds half asleep.

"It's Steph!"

"How's it going? Sorry, I was just in the bathroom."

"How long have you known about this?! About The Pink Coconut?"

"Well, hello, Stephanie. And it's lovely to hear from you, too."

"Come on, how long?"

"There will be other clubs, Steph."

"But not the Coconut! That was my home. That was my mainstay." I feel myself welling up, and will myself not to cry.

Tony seems nonplussed. "Well, you have bigger fish to fry now. You won't necessarily need the Coconut in future. Anyway, how's it going with the rapper? Filming going well?" says Tony, his voice *waaay* too cheery. "I heard from Candice that your son found you a new film crew. That was a stroke of luck, eh?"

What planet is this guy on?

"The rapper has not turned up, Tony."

Silence. Then a rustling of papers in the background.

"What day is it over there? Thursday? Shouldn't you be going to the gig, and then…? Hang on…"

More rustling of papers.

"Didn't you get the fax I sent you? I've got it in my hand right now. I'll read it to you…" Significant pause.

"*Dear Stephanie… please find enclosed schedule for your recording session with'*—"

"A fax?"

"Yes, a fax. With the schedule. Sent to the Lenox on Monday."

Oy vey! He sent a freaking fax? To the hotel we're not actually in? Seriously? Only Tony would send a fax like it was 1999.

"So, yes…" Tony continues, "'…*blah, blah, blah… Please find enclosed the planned schedule for your recording session with THE MOST*

FA'—"

"You couldn't have WhatsApped it to me?"

"Whats-what? Shall I just read it to you?" Tony says, sounding a bit more awake. He doesn't wait for my reply. "I'll just read it out, don't worry:

"Dear Stephanie, please find enclosed the planned schedule for your recording session with THE MOST FAMOUS RAPPER IN THE WORLD.' Right, okay... Tuesday... nope, that's gone... Wednesday... er, no... Ah, okay, yes... *Thursday night: attend previously unannounced gig with THE MOST FAMOUS RAPPER IN THE WORLD. Blah, blah, blah.... Afterwards, proceed with posse to do planned interviews with local radio stations about a joint single..."*

Oy. Freaking. Vey! Radio interviews? A secret gig?

"'After the interviews, THE MOST FAMOUS RAPPER IN THE WORLD and Stephanie to record radio drops with the same radio stations."

I could literally scream right now.

"Email it to me, Tony," I say, through gritted teeth. "Email it now, *pleeease!*" I add.

My head feels like it could explode at any moment; I could use some more painkillers. I root around in my purse for an Advil, taking things out and laying them on the table, until I see a loose pill at the bottom of my bag. I grab it and pop it straight in my mouth, washing it down with a gulp of Linus's water. It sticks in my throat; I take another big slug of water. And another. And another after that. Finally, after about five gulps it goes down. Damn, that was a seriously big pill to swallow.

A few minutes later, Linus comes sauntering back from the bathroom.

"So, are we going?" I say.

"Yeah, man, chill," he says. "I'll call the driver now."

Relief. Finally, I get to see Candice. I text Beaver.

"We're coming back to the hotel now!"

He doesn't reply.

I start to collect the contents of my bag from the table and pick up my iPad stylus. Where's the cover? I haven't put it back on. Must be in the bag. I root around for it and I re-empty the contents of my bag onto the table again: lipstick, bronzer, receipts and the Advil packet, which is… oh, my god – brand new and unopened!

But I just took a pill from that packet, didn't I? What?!

My throat suddenly feels sore. My stomach feels sick. I start to schvitz…

"O.M.G. Get me to a hospital!" I shriek.

So, it turns out you don't actually have to go to hospital if you've swallowed an iPad stylus cap. Apparently, if it goes down, it'll… er… well, it will eventually come out the other end. But the receptionist does suggest that I go to the local student health centre and talk to one of the nurses there, who can give me a mild laxative.

When we get there, the first person I see is Beaver, sitting in the waiting area. Beaver sees me and, not realizing his pun, the first words that come out of his mouth are: "Oh, crap." And then: "What are you doing here?"

"What am I doing here?!" I say, putting my hands on my hips. "I swallowed a freaking iPad stylus cap. What are YOU doing here?"

"Mmmm... I'm here with Candice. She fainted. Again. She's just being seen by the doctor."

"Fainted?"

"Yeah, she's not been feeling great: teary, nauseous... They think she's dehydrated."

Teary? Nauseous? Fainting?

Candice appears out of a side room. "Yeah, I'm pregnant," she says, slumping into a chair next to Beaver. She puts her head in her hands and bursts into tears.

"I'm sorry, Steph," she blurts out through the sobs, "I had no idea. I tried to hide it when I realized. Don't blame Beaver; I freaked and ran off; I didn't know what to do. I'm sorry. I didn't want to rain on your parade..."

"It's fine, sweetie, it's fine. You'll be okay," I say, shocked but only half-listening. I am distracted by the stack of email notifications, including this one, from Franz:

"SUBJECT: Sale of Café Michael — Term Sheet."

Chapter 10

"Who's The Daddy?"

"Dear Stephanie, please find the attached document, details of the terms of sale we have negotiated with B.C.W./KING AND QUEEN HOLDINGS LTD.

"The deal allows us to dispose of both assets, in London and New York, including transferring the leases on both properties and staff and to B.C.W. The company seeks to invest heavily in the business, commits to and continues to allow it to trade as a going concern.

"In my opinion, we would be mad to turn it down.

"Yours, as ever,

"Franz."

There is a ton of technical detail, but I sit in the Uber and read the email, re-reading one sentence over and over again:

"This allows us to dispose of the assets..."

It's not an asset. It's our family restaurant. It's a place where everyone meets. It's OUR place. It's not a fucking *asset!*

It IS an asset, honey, says the H.P.H. in my head, *and it kinda has to pay its way.*

But does that mean selling?

If it were me, yes, H.P.H. says.

I look over at Candice. She's been quiet on the short Uber ride through the campus, back to the hotel. Now she sits slumped in the seat, fiddling with her nails. Candice pregnant? I have so many questions – not least, WHO is the father?! Candice has ALWAYS had a lot of interest, but ever since she dumped that runner from *Strictly Come Dancing*, a few months back, I didn't think she'd actually had any significant others. Had she? Or is she planning on doing this all on her own?

I'm feeling a little in the dark, suddenly. I have gotten really close to Candice over the years. We've travelled together, and even shared hotel rooms on tour. I've met her folks on FaceTime a bunch of times, and been out for drinks with some of her besties. But, although Candice can be a regular chatterbox – confiding in me and asking for my advice on some very personal issues – we never, ever talked about her wanting to have kids right away, let alone be a single parent. It also feels that Candice would be considered quite young to have kids nowadays.

That said, I might be a teeny bit hypocritical, because I also got pregnant for the first time at only twenty-four. Okay, so I was already married, and living in a pretty cool but super-tiny apartment, on the Upper East Side of Manhattan – not too far to walk to Bloomingdale's, though barely enough room to swing a cat inside. Certainly no walk-in wardrobe; more keeping shoes in the stove, like Carrie in *Sex and the City*. Anyhow, K.C. and I wanted a large family so… hey, why wait?

I sigh. No matter whatever else I've tried to achieve in my life, being a mom is the freaking hardest job. And, in a few short months, Candice was going to find this out, too.

"O.M.G., I feel really sick," says Candice, suddenly. I yell at the driver to pull over quickly and, in the nick of time, Candice opens the door and throws up on the curb, spewing puke every which way.

We make a pit stop at the 7-11, to pick up some saltine crackers. My phone pings as I'm at the cash register: a message from my mother. *Please say that she hasn't seen the picture of me with the cops, too?!* I'm really hoping that will just disappear quietly. Nope, just a blurry image; I'm not sure I can even see what it actually is. Looks like the Tesco Express by Gloucester Road tube station.

Another message pings in, almost immediately afterwards:

"You see, Stephanie?"

"No, I really can't, actually, Mom," I type back.

Alejandro laughs at this when we FaceTime later on.

"What do you think the picture was?" he asks.

"My mom says it's Beverly. Says she's up to something."

"Up to something? Cuddly old Beverly? C'mon."

"I know!" I say. "My mom can be so dramatic. I'm so glad

you agree!"

"Well," says Alejandro, sensibly, "I'm bringing Constanza over to yours tomorrow, for a playdate with Emily, so I'll talk to your Mom then." He takes a large mouthful of wine from a bulbous glass.

"So, come on, then, tell me about the rapper," he says. "Is he as hot in real life as he looks on T.V.?"

"I haven't met him yet," I confess.

"WHAT?!"

"Please, just leave it."

"That's the only reason you went out there!" Alejandro says, arms flailing, chardonnay splashing about. "You're on the clock, honey; you need to seal the deal. Find the rapper. Sing the rap – or whatever you're meant to do with rap. Seal. The. Freaking. Deal!"

"It's complicated," I say, eventually. "But I spoke to Tony and apparently he's got it under control," I say, hopeful that he wasn't bullshitting me. "Plus, I learned LOADS about spicy sauce."

"O.M.G., Steph," says Alejandro. "Spicy sauce?! You're meant to come back with the hit record."

I'm silent for a moment. "Well, what does it matter anymore? The only club I play on a regular basis is closing," I say, sulkily.

Alejandro stops and takes another gulp of wine. "I'm so sorry, Steph. I think they just didn't make it out of the pandemic… like—"

"Like the restaurants?"

"I was going to say, 'like so many'. Sorry, Steph, I know how much—"

I stare down at my feet. "They've got a buyer," I say, in a small voice, "for the restaurants. Franz wants me to sign before the weekend."

"Oh, well, that's good, no?"

"No, it's not," I snap.

"But, Steph," he says, soothingly, "you know you have to sell."

"Let's change the subject," I say.

"Okay," says Al, clearly frustrated. "What else is going on?"

"Candice is pregnant."

"What the…?! Who? How? I mean, I know how, but who?"

I shrug. I have no idea.

Alejandro blows out his cheeks. "Well, that's news. Not sure I can top that." He pauses, then smiles mischievously. "Or maybe I can…?"

"Go on."

"Well, you will NEVER guess who I spied at Harry's Bar the other day, having lunch with the Bitch of Belgravia…?"

"WHO? WHO?! Another man? Tell me!!!" I'm freaking out. Wachman gossip is gold.

"Nope. Guess again."

"Her trainer? The really hot one?"

"No. I'll tell you." He leans into the screen. "Christina Wachman was with... the school headmistress."

"Oh. That's dull," I say, totally unimpressed. "Wachman and Mrs. Smart? Who cares?"

"But weird, all the same?" says Alejandro, eyes narrowing. "I mean, who hangs out with the school's headmistress, at one of the most expensive private clubs in London? Especially *that* headmistress; everyone knows she's a tricky customer. The only thing I can think is that Lucas got bad grades."

"I doubt it," I say, thinking: *If that were the case, they'd have met in her office, NOT Harry's Bar.* Besides, like most High Performing Chelsea kids, Lucas Wachman wouldn't DARE get bad grades.

"Well, be the doubting Thomas if you will," Alejandro continues, "but, when I went over, Wachman went bright red. She was totally embarrassed to be spotted."

"Weird," I say, still not particularly interested. It's not even juicy gossip.

Though, I still can't shake the feeling that Lucas's mother is somehow behind Logan getting kicked off the football team. Now, I don't like calling any woman "the B word", but Alejandro's nickname for Christina Wachman – "the Bitch of Belgravia" – is pretty accurate. The thing with Wachman is that it's her way or no way. Her children must be the best and most successful, her dresses the most current and most expensive, her holidays the most far-flung. It's sharp elbows that count in

Wachman's world, not the Sisterhood. I heard one particularly hideous story about a midweek dinner party at the Wachmans', where one guest left in the pouring rain and couldn't get a taxi. She returned to the house like a drowned rat, and one of the male guests offered to drop her back on his own way home. Then Wachman had the biggest hissy fit, in front of EVERYONE, about how the man couldn't possibly leave to help someone else, because he originally offered to stay behind to walk her dog for her. I mean, honestly?! I like dogs, but COME ON…! Walk her dog?! W.T.A.F.? Her guest was stranded! That woman is a nasty piece of work, and she'll do ANYTHING to get her and her kids ahead.

"Anyhow," says Alejandro, "who's the buyer, anyway?"

"Does it matter, if it's just about the money?"

"Of course it matters."

"Some dude called B.C.W. Holdings. Never heard of them."

I've known Alejandro for a long time. And there would have been a time when it would have been ME telling HIM a few home truths. He's Canadian, too (although his Mom is from England), and we met back at college. He was studying Interior Design and Fine Arts at Ryerson University in Toronto. We reconnected when he moved over to London, to be with his girlfriend. I know what you're thinking: his GIRLFRIEND?! Ruby was twenty-six, English, five-foot-eight, size six and absolutely freaking gorgeous. Alejandro had moved to London to be with her, as she'd got a job doing something in finance, in the City. They had the perfect apartment in Chelsea and even got a dog: a Cockerpoo called Leonard. To the outside they were a gorgeous, successful, upwardly-mobile London couple. Only problem, of course, was that Alejandro was actually gay. That was his secret...

...or so he thought. For those of us who knew him well, it was obvious. He just didn't fancy her. Beaver had figured it out, of course, and even H.P.H, who didn't have any kind of functioning gaydar, made some comments after bumping into him at his gym, as Alejandro was coming out of a Zumba class. But it was definitely obvious to me. The only problem now was: should I tell him that I know? At that time, the fact that I was getting to know the gay scene through my music was actually a blessing. I'd have a gig at a gay club and ask Alejandro along to support me... and he'd inevitably find a guy he thought was super-hot, then he'd totally deny it.

But, back at home, Ruby was upping the ante. She wanted to get married and, despite all the hints and the constant trips to Tiffany's, to look at something "cute", which she'd "just seen online", Alejandro just wasn't putting a ring on it.

He finally confessed to me, over cocktails and sushi one evening. He picked up his chopsticks, toyed with a California roll, said he felt trapped and started to cry.

"I can't do it, Steph!" he said, sobbing into a bowl of

edamame beans. "I can't marry her!"

"Honey," I said, putting my hand on his shoulder, "do you think the reason you don't want to marry Ruby is because you're gay?"

His relief exploded into more tears – tears of relief, I believe. Then both of us hugged and sobbed, then hugged some more.

Ruby and Alejandro split up shortly afterwards.

To be honest, I was always surprised that Ruby didn't know he was gay. Maybe she just thought he had that "European flair". After Ruby's initial shock, and a few recriminations, it was a pretty amicable parting. Certainly more amicable than most Chelsea breakups I've known.

They made a profit when they sold the apartment, and split the artworks and Le Creuset kitchenware straight down the middle. She took the dog. Last I heard, Ruby had gotten engaged to a farming veterinarian and moved to Cornwall. Meanwhile, Alejandro, who I emotionally supported with trips shopping, clubbing and to the best spas in Knightsbridge, got busy having the freakin' time of his life on Grindr. Then, a year or so later, he met and settled down with the great Mayfair hedge-fund manager Timothy Green.

Maybe he's right, though. Maybe I do need to sell.

Just as I hang up with my bestie, there is a loud ping from my phone: another message from my mother. It's just another bloody picture! I stare at the grainy image. Looks like another snap from the streets of Kensington: a tall woman in a coat and some other guy. *What the fuck, Mom?*

I type back: *"Great pics, Mom. xx. Hope the kids are OK."*

"Kids are fine. Stephanie, these are NOT great pictures!"

"You think?!" I scream at the phone. *Jeez! What. Is. My. Mother. On?!*

Instead of checking out homebound melodrama, I should be putting my time into writing new top lines and lyrics for another track I've been working on. With that in mind, I pop my headphones on and search on my iPad for the beats my producers transferred over. I listen to it and start to scribble lyrics onto a notepad. After a few lines, I start to feel so energized by the thumping dance beat, I start dancing around in my room.

I need a Diet Coke. Vending machine.

Outside in the corridor, I see Linus, nonchalant as fuck, smoking a cigarette. W.T.F.! Can't he see the *"No Smoking"* signs? Surely that thing is going to set off the sprinklers, then everyone will have to get up – including Candice, who really shouldn't be getting up right now.

"Hey, Li!" I call out, and feign smoking a cigarette to accentuate my point. "Put that thing out, dude! You'll set off the sprinklers!"

He looks around and tips his head back, to acknowledge he's seen me, then takes another drag on the cigarette.

"Hey, Steph, how's it going?" He fishes the packet out of his jacket pocket and offers me one. "You want?"

O.M.F.G.! I am SO angry, I literally smash the packet out of his hands. "What the fuck, Li? No, I don't want one. You can't smoke in here!"

"Chill, man," Linus says, stooping down to pick up the packet off the grimy carpet. "Z-Drive already turned the sprinklers off, man. I'm just gonna finish smoking this, then we all gonna go for some drinks. You wanna come?"

"Linus," I say, "you know, honestly, I'd love to, but I really want to sleep. Plus I have to ask you: am I actually ever going to get to record with THE MOST FAMOUS RAPPER IN THE WORLD?"

Linus ignores the question. "Hey, no problem, little lady. Still jetlagged, huh? You on London time, eh? I'm just gonna wait here for Z and the rest of the crew." He takes yet another drag on the cigarette, which weirdly has not set off an alarm or sprinklers. Guess they really must have switched them off again.

"Linus… I really think we need to talk about this whole—" I start to say, wanting to try and see whether the elusive rapper might be anywhere near the building, but then my phone starts buzzing in my pocket: my mother is on FaceTime. What does she want now?

"Mom? Are you okay?" I say. "It's late and I'm a bit busy. And what's with these pic—"

"Stephanie, I need to talk to you. You need to come home."

"What? Mom, what's the problem? It can't be that bad."

My mother gives me one of her special withering looks, one I can feel all the way from across the pond, and I instantly regress to the age of fifteen.

"Are those real problems, Stephanie? Are they problems that affect your family or your children? Or just problems that affect STAR Roberts's life?"

"Mom!!! Of course they are real problems!" I say, starting to get pissed and also suspicious, because she has always refused to use my stage name… or, when she does, she almost always gets it wrong. There was even one memorable occasion when she announced me to her bridge friends as: "Stash Roberts, the singer."

"Mom, you know the situation: I need to record this track, do the video then get back to London – and we still haven't recorded."

"Whyever not, Stephanie? You've been there for DAYS now!"

"I know, Mom," I sigh, "but THE MOST FAMOUS RAPPER IN THE WORLD hasn't turned up yet."

"HASN'T TURNED UP?!" my mother roars. "Does this man understand about timekeeping?"

"No, Mom, they don't know about that," I say.

My mother seems to soften momentarily. "Right, honey,

who's in charge there?" she asks.

"Ermmm, Linus, I guess," I say, wondering if in fact anyone in this crew is actually in charge.

"Okay, good," my mother says. "Put him on the phone with me, right now."

"Er, Linus?" I beckon him over, "my mother would like a word."

He is still smoking his cigarette and he hands it to me, so that he can hold the phone and peer at the pissed seventy-year-old, now staring daggers back at him. I literally want to crawl into a hole and die.

"Well, hello, Linus," I hear my mother say. "My name is Bubby. I'm Stephanie's mother."

O.M.G.! THIS. IS. THE. END. OF. ANY. STREET. CRED. I. EVER. HAD!

"Yes, ma'am," Linus says, looking directly at the screen. "Hello, Mrs. Bubby."

"Right, well, you look like a perfectly respectable and nice man," my mother continues. "In fact, I would say you have particularly kind eyes. Now, could you tell me where, exactly, is this person my daughter calls THE MOST FAMOUS RAPPER IN THE WORLD?"

"Well, he ain't here right now, Mrs. Bubby," Linus says, shifting from foot to foot.

"Well, WHERE is he?"

"I can't tell you, Mrs. Bubby."

"Whyever not?

Linus pauses for a moment, like a child trying to come up with a plausible excuse for why there aren't any more cookies in the cookie jar. "That's confidential, Mrs. Bubby, ma'am."

My mother does one of her famous harrumphs. "Do you *know* where he is?"

"I can't tell you that, Mrs. Bubby, ma'am."

"Right. I see. Thank you. Would you give the phone back to my daughter, please?"

"Yes, ma'am, Mrs. Bubby, ma'am." Linus swiftly hands me the phone, grabs the butt of the cigarette out of my fingers and turns on his heel. I am literally dying right now.

My mother is looking serious. Oy vey! I *reaaaaallly* hate it when this happens.

"It's just tricky, Mom," I start to say. "He's a BIG rapper, a huge star; he's busy. Schedules change. You know, I can wait a bit longer. It's super-important."

My mother is just looking at me. A terrifying, *Silence of the Lambs*, "I'm-about-to-kill-you" kind of glare. It's just like that night when I called her and told her I'd met the man I was going to marry, except now it's on freaking FaceTime, and it's even worse. I'm starting to hope the entire internet breaks, and we all have to go back to writing letters instead.

"Stephanie," says my mother, shaking her head, "this rapper

man is not coming. This is all one big old pipe dream. You need to get on a plane and come home to your family."

Except, the thing is, I'm not twenty-one anymore; I'm forty-two. I'm widowed. A mother of three children, who is juggling a somewhat successful singing career... And, this time – although she's playing the "holier-than-thou" card – it's my mother gallivanting with a new man I know nothing about, and having obsessive-compulsive suspicions over my Mary Poppins nanny. Suddenly I start to feel very, very angry.

"No, Mom!" I say, furiously. "I've waited forty-two years for this. I have lost my husband; I have lost the family business. I am not freaking coming home!"

Chapter 11

"Frenemy"

"Stephanie, you need to take this deal seriously. If we're going to sign, then we need to do so before the weekend."

It's the next morning and I am lying in bed, sun streaming in through the curtains. And through the gap I can see that the sky is a deep, bright blue. I'm not really listening to what Franz is saying. I hold the phone away from my ear. I don't want to engage with what he's telling me.

"Franz, I'm not doing it right now," I say, resting on my elbows and pulling the duvet around my shoulders. "You've got to wait 'til I get home. I need to think about this."

"There's not much to think about, Steph, and I don't see what the problem is. Mr. Wachman is adamant that he wants this deal signed by the weekend, otherwise, he's out."

I sit bolt upright.

Wachman?!

"I'm sorry?"

"Mr. Benjamin Wachman, B.C.W. Holdings. I believe you know him personally."

What. The. Actual. Fuck?!

Thirty minutes later, I'm running fast on the treadmill in the hotel's shitty gym. The Wachmans are trying to buy Café Michael? Are they even serious? Is this some kind of awful joke?

Did you know about this? I ask H.P.H. silently, my feet pounding down on the treadmill. But, for once, he doesn't reply; there is silence. He and Benjamin were friends, for sure. Good friends. Always there for each other, in business and personally. But, buying Café Michael? *The Wachmans owning my ass? Not one bloody chance in Hell!*

I do miss playing golf with Wachie. We had such fun times together, says H.P.H. *I think it's absolutely fine.*

Ya, I know you liked him, babe, but he's a bit of a lady's man, no? I say back.

Well... one, that doesn't come into it when business is involved, says H.P.H., *and, two, if you were married to her... wouldn't you be looking at other chicks?*

I run faster, my heart rate increasing, breathing deeper to get the oxygen pumping around. Being active, keeping fit and in shape is part of my daily routine... and, ever since I was young, I've loved everything related to fitness. I was quite a plump pubescent, so it's a darn good thing I became obsessed with working out. In fact, when I was seventeen, I took a year-long course to learn how to teach aerobics. By the time I was nineteen, I was teaching over twenty classes a week, all around Ottawa, and I'd saved up enough cash to travel around Europe with my childhood bestie, Charlotte – also a fitness fanatic. Over the years I've learned to work out anywhere: on planes, on boats, even in the odd taxi. Getting the blood pumping is how I stay feeling strong and sane. I'm not sure it's working today.

The Wachmans want to buy my family's restaurant. The *Wachmans!* I can't stop thinking about it.

An hour later, I throw on a hoodie and jacket, and make a trip to the 7-11, to pick up some bananas and yoghurt. The figures are going round and round in my head. It's a great offer; any sane person would take it. I do not feel sane right now.

I'm by the cash register when my phone starts buzzing. Emily's bright, smiling face appears on the FaceTime screen, and I can't help but smile when I see it. She does the gangsta rapper handshake thing into the air and, even without a partner's hand to slide and pump, it still looks way cooler than how I do it.

"Hi, Mom! How's it going with the rapper?" she says.

Oh, God. I've been so obsessed with thinking about the Café Michael sale, I'd forgotten about how badly that was going.

"Hi, honey!" I say, pinching the phone between my ear and shoulder, as I gather up the bananas and yoghurt. "Oh, it's going great! I'll be home soon."

"Mom... really?" Emily narrows her eyes. "Constanza told me he hasn't turned up yet."

"How does she know that?"

"Her dad told her." I should realize that, by telling Alejandro anything, I'm practically telling Emily.

"Well, okay, he hasn't just yet. But he's definitely coming today, and then I'll be home," I say, feeling momentarily guilty about telling a little white lie to my daughter because, the way this has been going, I'm not sure he really will ever turn up. And then I notice she isn't where she's meant to be, either.

"Honey, that's OUR kitchen!" I say suddenly, clocking the scene. "Are you at home? Why aren't you at school?"

"Er, snow day, Mom!" She flips the camera toward the back garden, to reveal a light, white dusting on the lawn. "Can you believe it? They cancelled school for that!" she says, grinning. "Apparently, the tube and buses aren't running 'cuz it's too icy; the teachers were having trouble getting in…" she rolls her eyes, "…if you believe that."

I chuckle, thinking back to my childhood in Canada. If they'd cancelled school every time it snowed there, I'd have never had an education!

"So, is Costanza there now?"

"Ya, she's here with Al, because Beverly had to go somewhere."

"What? Beverly's not there? Where's she gone?"

"I dunno, Mom? Alejandro is here, though."

"Where's Bubby?"

"She went out, too."

"Went out?" I have a vision of my mother slipping in the

street and breaking her hip. "How about Gerald?"

"Mmmm, don't know, Mom. I think he might still be in the hospital, or maybe he went to the doctor for a check-up. I really don't know; I've literally only just met the guy. Mom, can I go now?"

"Put Alejandro on."

"ALEJANDRO!!!!!!!!" screams Emily, so loudly I move the phone away from my face. "My mom wants to talk to YOU!"

Alejandro's face pops into view.

"O.M.G.," I say, "I'm so sorry you're stuck there with the kids in the middle of the day! Where the hell is Beverly?"

Alejandro shrugs. "No worries, Steph. We were all thrown off by this snow day! So, we just brought the after-school playdate forward. Beverly's fine. She said she had to pop out for a few minutes. She'll be back soon enough, then I'll go. Anyway, Steph, any sign of the rapper?"

"No."

"Okay." Alejandro looks at me sideways. "But there's something else, isn't there?"

"No."

"There's something else. I know it!"

"Okay, so there might be something else."

"What is it?" asks Alejandro, his eyes wide. "Did you find out why Mrs. Smart was meeting with Wachman?"

"No."

"Oh, come on."

I can't bring myself to say it.

"Stephanie… Come on, tell Uncle Al…"

"It's the Wachmans," I say, in a small voice.

"So, it *is* about the Wachmans! I knew it! What do you know? What's going on with Mrs. Smart? I knew there was something suspicious there. I knew it! I knew it!"

"No, it's nothing to do with that... and, for the record, Al, I really don't understand why you're so obsessed with that. They want to buy Café Michael – well, Benjamin Wachman does; his investment fund does. They're B.C.W. Holdings."

"Oh."

"Exactly."

"Well, I suppose their money is as good as anyone else's, babe."

"They're not gonna have it," I say, my voice as petulant as a seven-year-old child in the midst of a snit-fit.

"Oh, come on, Steph. If it's a good deal—"

"No, they're not having Café Michael," I say sharply. "I'm not doing it."

"I think you might be cutting off your nose to spite your face, Steph."

"Not a chance in Hell!" I say.

And, with that pissy declaration, I cut off the FaceTime.

Beaver and Candice are sitting in the restaurant when I get back to the hotel. Candice is eating pancakes.

"Hey!" I say, as upbeat as I can muster, skipping over to the booth where they're sitting. "Not feeling nauseous today?"

"Nope, not today, thank God," Candice smiles, pushing another forkful of pancake and syrup into her mouth. "I guess the good thing is that I can eat anything I like now," she says. "Eating for two, and all that."

I bite my tongue and choose not to tell her that a pregnant woman actually only needs an extra three hundred calories a day – of *healthy* food!

"Yeah, you can, but not soft cheeses and pâté," says Beaver. "Although, most sushi is okay; I Googled it last night. They freeze the fish first, so it kills all the parasitic worms."

Candice makes a half-terrified, half-*"ewww, yuck"* face. Beaver changes the subject.

"So…" he asks, "is today gonna be the day?"

"Yep, sure is," I beam. "This is going to be the day! I just know it."

Of course it is, I tell myself. Truth is, we haven't got many days left.

I sit down next to them, pour myself a coffee and look at my phone. It's been blowing up with messages ever since I killed the FaceTime on Al. They are all from my mother. Image after image after image streams onto my phone.

They're slightly less blurred than the images she sent before, and this time I recognize the woman: it's Beverly. Beverly at a cashpoint. Beverly at a till, at the Gloucester Road Tesco Express. Beverly going into a pub...? Beverly hugging a young man outside the pub?!

Seconds later, my mother is calling.

"Stephanie," my mother says breathlessly, not even bothering to say hello, "I have just followed your nanny to the cashpoint!"

Okay, my mother is literally insane.

"What, Mom?" I say. "You followed Beverly? What? Why?"

"Because she's stealing from you!"

What the hell has she been smoking?

My mother repeats herself: "Stephanie Rachel Bloom, your nanny is a criminal!"

OKAY! Enough now!

"Mom, please, just listen to me," I say. "Beverly has been living with us for almost three years now. She lives IN OUR HOME. She travels with us. She never gets sick. She's brilliant at cooking. She's always charged a reasonable amount, and never once talked about upping her fees. The kids adore her. She is the best freaking nanny I ever had. Mom, I trust that woman with my life. No, more than that: I trust her with my kids' lives!"

"But the money... so much money!" my mother rants. "I saw it with my own eyes! Wads and wads of it! And then to the pub!

Like… like some kind of a drug dealer!"

"Mom," I say wearily, "she ALWAYS withdraws cash. She needs to buy food, to buy stuff for the kids, things at the drugstore, cleaning supplies... She was getting new football shorts for Logan and stationery for Emily this week," I say, in defence of our wonderful Beverly Poppins.

"Not that much cash, Steph! Check your bloody bank statements, please! I also saw her rooting around in your room, near your jewellery case, last night. Gerald finds her very strange, and believes she may well have some kind of personality disorder."

"Oh, Mom, stop," I say. "Gerald is over eighty, and on high-strength blood-pressure-lowering tablets and beta blockers, which I'm pretty sure have slowed his powers of rational thought. Plus, I haven't actually met him, so I'm not sure I'm going to take his opinion all that seriously yet."

"Stephanie," my mother shakes her head, "it's no good. You need to come home. Now."

To add insult to injury, I am starting to itch everywhere again, underneath my gym kit. What the hell is going on here? Is my mother now winding me up so much it's making me itch? I scratch across my chest, leaving angry, red marks on my skin. Fantastic.

"Mom," I say, scratching furiously, "you already said that, but I'm not, okay? I'm going now. Goodbye."

I look down at my chest: it's red and inflamed. *Are there fleas in my bed or something?*

Linus comes lumbering past the table. "Hey, man," he says. "You been working out?"

"Yeah, always!" I say, forcing a broad smile, slipping my phone into my pocket and hoping that he doesn't notice the red bumps on my cleavage. I would just have to add that to my ever-growing list of cred-killers, like my mother's tirade last night.

Candice reaches over and grabs my hand, excitedly. "He's back, babe!" she whispers in my ear. "Today really is going to be the day!"

My heart starts to beat faster. She's right! And that means the posse will be, too. Surely.

I suddenly remember what Tony said about the concert and the radio drops. He'd sent the email but – typical Tony – no actual details of place or time. God, is it today? I have to find out where it is. I stand up and call after Linus, but he's gone already. *Dammit!*

Franz is texting me again:

"Any more thoughts about the deal, Stephanie? I'd like to get this moving."

I delete the text and drink some more coffee.

By late afternoon, we're still hanging out in the hotel. We have done virtually nothing all day. The place is deserted; no one has seen Linus or any of the posse. I check the email again but, as I thought, no details. *F.F.S.! I'm calling Tony.*

"Hey, Tone," I say, when he eventually picks up. "Secret gig – it's tonight. I got the email; no details on where, though. This is a problem. Give me the low down."

"Oh, okay, right, right." I hear a rustling of paper at the end of the line. "Er… right…: *'blah, blah, blah, blah, blah…'* No, get down, get down! No, Malcolm, I can't take you for walkies at the moment. Yes…"

"Tony, come on! Details? Please?"

More rustling.

"Right. It says here that the concert is at… oh, *'location T.B.C.'…*"

Okay. Unknown location. Fantastic.

"Is there a time?" I say, moving over to the window, peeling back the net curtains and spotting what looks to be Z-Drive helping someone carry a huge, black box toward a large minivan, out front of the Hotel Du Slum. The film crew – who've become a law unto themselves – follow him.

I open the window and yell out to Josh, the pip-squeak director: "Hey, what are you doing down there?!"

He squints and puts his hand behind his ear, to indicate that he can't hear what I'm yelling.

"I'll text you!!!!" I yell back, even louder. He nods

noncommittally.

"Erm, Stephanie, are you still listening?" Tony is saying in my ear. "So, it says here that THE MOST FAMOUS RAPPER IN THE WORLD is on stage at ten p.m., but the warm-up act starts at eight."

I take the phone away from my ear and look at my watch: eight p.m. is in a couple of hours' time. I text Josh: *"DO NOT LET Z-DRIVE OUT OF YOUR SIGHT! FIND OUT WHERE THE CONCERT IS!!!!"*

I see that Josh has read the text, and look up to find Candice in floods of tears on the bed. Beaver is comforting her.

"I just don't know whether I should go to the concert, you know?" I hear her saying. "I mean, I absolutely LOVE the MOST FAMOUS RAPPER IN THE WORLD, and I just love everything about him... and a s-s-s-secret c-c-concert... but... but the, the, the baby – is it good for the baby? Can I go to a concert? A loud music concert?" She fans her face dramatically.

"I'm sure it will be fine, darl'," Beaver says, in full-on counselling mode. "Do you know, I think they did research on concerts: I think music calms the growing baby; makes it more intelligent or something. I'm sure I read it in a magazine."

"I think that was Mozart," I say. "But this kid is not being born into the eighteenth century, so I'd say you and the little one will be absolutely fine, at eight weeks' gestation, with a bit of light gangsta rap. Just maybe don't do any shots afterwards, eh?" I joke, trying to lighten the mood. "You know what I was told: you gotta treat your first like you'd treat your fourth."

Candice looks at me and sniffs. "But I've never done it before, so how do I know how to do any of it? And, Steph, how would you even know how to treat a fourth; you've only got three?"

"It'll be fine. You're doing so great, Candice, sweetheart," Beaver says, and places his hand protectively over Candice's stomach.

"Yeah, I guess so. I just feel *soooo* emotionally drained at the moment." She flops into Beaver's arms.

Oy vey. Me too, honey, I think. *Except I'm way closer to the menopause than you are, girl.*

"Are you still there, Steph?" a voice from across the Atlantic wafts out of my phone.

I snap back into concentration. "Sorry, Tony. Yes."

"So, anyway, afterwards… *'blah, blah, blah…'* It says here that you and THE MOST FAMOUS RAPPER IN THE WORLD are going to do some radio interviews about the new single, and radio drops with local stations, and then… Oh, yes!" says Tony. "And THEN they're going to set up a studio at the concert venue, and you'll record the new single there."

And there it is: the answer to the million-dollar question I've been asking this entire week. Just have to find out where this unknown location is. *O-KAY… Freaking brilliant!* I do not say this, of course.

Instead, I say: "Sounds fabulous, Tony!"

"Glad to be of help, Star," Tony says. "But now, if you'll excuse me, I really must go and walk Malcolm. Go get 'em, girl!"

I put down the phone in a bit of a daze.

Beaver jumps up and does a little scream. "Righty-ho, gorgeous! What look are we going for tonight, babes?" He pulls over his large make-up case. "Come here, my darling!" he says, wafting his make-up brushes in my face. "Let's get you READY TO RAP!"

Beaver stops suddenly, as I move toward him.

"Hang on. What the fuck is that on your chest?" Beaver says, stopping short as he catches sight of my red, raw chest.

"Oy, just an itch," I say.

"Looks like you've got fleas, love," Beaver replies. "Well, that can't do. Let's get some cover-up on that."

Candice smiles weakly from the bed, still dabbing her eyes, as Beaver starts to sort out bottles and tubes. *Poor Candice,* I think, scratching again at my chest. I'm not sure it's fair to tell her that the pregnancy is the easy bit.

Josh turns up at the door a few minutes later, with Z-Drive. "I thought it best to bring him to you," he says breathlessly; "hear it from the horse's mouth, and all that."

Beaver is just sticking on my eyelashes, but stops and stands back so I can talk to Z-Drive.

"Has anyone seen Linus?" I ask, although I expect I already know the answer.

"Li? He at the sound check, yo," says Z-Drive. "You coming too, Sista?"

I'm trying to.

"Of course!" I say. "I just totally forgot where it was. Do you have the address?"

"It's at the college, yo. Yeah?"

"Which college? And where, exactly?"

Z-Drive shifts from foot to foot and says: "I dunno, but the minivan driver, he knows, yo."

He disappears and reappears a few minutes later, with a piece of paper, on which has been scrawled the name of a university building and zip code. I look at it, trying to discern the numerals.

"*'Atlantis Building, Hunt Street...'* Is that a one or a seven?" I say, showing Z-Drive the paper.

"Seven?" he says, hopefully. "Yeah, I reckon, definitely. Seven's my lucky number."

"Z-Drive," I say, throwing him a winning, cheerleader-worthy smile. "I know we'll have to ride in the back of the van, but this time can we just come with you?"

My mother calls me again on the way to the concert. I decline it. Unless one of my kids is haemorrhaging or in jail, I do not want to hear about it right now. I am laser-focused on the fact that I am finally heading to the place where THE MOST FAMOUS RAPPER IN THE WORLD is going to be. And, in less than a few hours' time, I am *ACTUALLY* going to be recording with him, after doing promotional interviews and radio drops. *YAY!*

Beaver has done an amazing job on my look: Dolce and Gabbana glittery-gold dress; sky-high Louboutins, and a buttery-soft leather jacket I picked up in a cute boutique in St. Tropez. I'm rocking super-long eyelashes, smoky eyes and a slick of bright-red lipstick. I've gone off the whole "red-lipstick-makes-me-look-like-my-mother" schtick because, I have to admit, I look HOT (although, I am most certainly going to freeze my tuchus off when I step outside in the snow, to get to the venue)! I check out my glittery gel nails and take a cleansing breath.

Okay, so we are all sitting amongst the stage boxes in the back of a windowless transporter van, but, you know, it's cool. This is rock 'n' roll. Or gangsta rap. Yes, this is most definitely gangsta.

"Don't even ask me to go and get some milk or snacks, or anything that a normal person might do right now!" I joke with Josh, as the van turns another corner and we all hang on for dear life.

"Ha!" says Josh. "Good point: we probably should be filming this. It's great television."

I shoot Josh a withering look.

"Oh, c'mon, Steph," he says, trying his luck and indicating to

Toby to pick up the camera. "We can always edit you out."

Anyone who is passionate about performing will tell you there is something incredible about walking onto an empty stage, in the hours before the auditorium fills. The place just buzzes with energy. THE MOST FAMOUS RAPPER IN THE WORLD's people are running around, unpacking boxes and bags, setting the stage up, plugging in microphones and arranging amplifiers. There are the characteristic squeaks and squawks as sound systems are tested.

THE MOST FAMOUS RAPPER IN THE WORLD's musicians and backing singers arrive, unpacking their instruments and smoothing their hair.

"Oh, it's so incredible," Candice says.

I smile at her and give her a big hug. "It sure is," I say, a humongous smile spreading across my face. It's really happening.

I can feel my phone buzzing in my clutch bag. *Oy vey, I bet it's my mother!*

"Can you look after that?" I say, handing the bag to Candice. I'm not letting anything distract me. I just want to enjoy the experience and focus on the next few hours, which I just know will be amazing.

And it is! The place is packed with students and the atmosphere is buzzing.

The opening act is a young rapper from L.A., on the same label as THE MOST FAMOUS RAPPER IN THE WORLD. He is debuting his new single and, I gotta say, it is pretty good.

The "opening act" is a nerve-wracking slot, because your job is to hype the crowd to super-excited mode, and it can TOTALLY go tits-up if they don't like you. I remember the time I was opening for Billy Ocean, at the Formula One races in Silverstone. I had four gorgeous girl dancers with me, and had taken my son Logan to the gig, too, because he was so into race cars at the time, and I thought it would be fun for him to see the action live. So, I was really nervous because these were people into race-car driving and, while they were probably happy to hear Billy Ocean sing his hit tune "Caribbean Queen" live, they might not have been so keen about dance music. But Tony was having none of my negativity, saying it would be a great promo opportunity to really "get my name out there", and would only "happen when the new album comes out." Then, just before I was about to go on, someone in the P.R. department came over to offer Logan the chance to meet race-car driver Lewis Hamilton, back in the pit. But he politely turned down the opportunity, because he didn't want to miss my show. I told Logan he should go and meet Lewis Hamilton; he could always see me perform. But he said: "Mom, I'm here for YOU. You need me, not Lewis Hamilton."

Now, that is one awesome moment of son support.

I totally brought the house down that day, and my kid was seriously impressed when a bunch of fans came around back to get my autograph and take selfies with me.

"Er, Steph…" Candice waves my iPhone at me, "your mom has called four times now. I think you should probably reply."

Suddenly, all the lights go dark. The crowd starts to whoop and cheer. It's dark and still for a moment, then a single spotlight lights up… and he's there: THE MOST FAMOUS RAPPER IN THE WORLD is ON STAGE!

I slip the phone back into my pocket. I'll deal with my mother later.

Back on stage… my god, this guy knows how to grab an audience and hold on tight.

He performs hit after hit. Z-Drive is on the keyboards and even the security guys are there; the whole posse is on stage, or in the pit in front. And then, THE MOST FAMOUS RAPPER IN THE WORLD starts freestyling something he introduces as "A Worcester State of Mind":

"Yeah, yeah…
Worcester!! Worriers!! It's time.
Time, yo,
To draw the line.

This beat, uh – it's got the power.

"We grind for justice; it's been a minute,
Spitting truth, no gimmicks, we livin' in it.
Take to the streets, but it seems in vain;
They ignore our pain, won't accept the blame,
From Tupac to Kendrick Lamar,
From Erykah Badu to Nas' bars,
Rhymes been our weapon, our protest,
Our way of saying, we won't be oppressed,
This is how we express the struggle,
'Nough's enough; no more hustle.

"From the East to the West, let's raise our voice;
It's time to stand up, time to make a choice.
From the ghetto, the burbs, the penthouse, the glory,
We all got a struggle, we all got a story.
The beat of the street can change the game –
It can heal the pain, it can break the chains, it can bring the
fame…"

I sit back and close my eyes. This guy – he is beyond *amaaaazing!* I cannot believe how lucky I am to be recording with him, and have him actually writing a rap with me. He is mesmerizing. Z-Drive and Linus are at the back of the stage, arms aloft, waving their hands, and the audience is going wild. And I am there in the wings, watching, just a few feet away from my hero. Candice, Beaver and I are leaping around at the back of the stage, loving every moment. I couldn't be happier right now; I am literally in Heaven.

THE MOST FAMOUS RAPPER IN THE WORLD performs for about an hour and a half, and the crowd goes insane. There's encore after encore after encore, then finally he and the rest of the posse take a final bow.

The applause peters out and I watch as the audience start to pick up their bags and coats, move toward the exits and file out.

We're still hanging around in the wings when Linus comes over.

"You ready?" he says.

"Linus," I say, putting my hands on my hips, "I have never been more ready in my life."

I look over at Beaver, who is whispering something into Candice's ear. I beckon them over and say: "Radio interviews now. You coming?"

"I think, if you don't mind, I'm going to take Candice home," Beaver says, then adds, "obviously I'll touch up your make-up first."

"I don't want to let you down, Steph," Candice says, looking uncomfortable, "but I'm feeling quite tired, and I still feel quite sick." She does look exhausted. It must be almost midnight.

"OF COURSE!" I say, doing my best to appear like I don't mind. "Yes, go, go. You don't need to stay here; I've got the film crew. We'll all come back together after the interviews and the recording."

"Okay, if you're sure," says Candice, looking at her feet.

"Yes! Go, go! Get some sleep! We'll have this wrapped in a jiffy and I'll be back at the hotel. I mean, c'mon, you don't need to be there; you're not the one singing," I say, shooing them away.

Beaver gives me a hug and a hopeless shrug, as if to say, "I really need to go with her," before they both head out. I watch as they leave the auditorium.

Linus suddenly taps me on the shoulder, making me jump. "Your crew not coming wit' you?"

"Nope, just me and the film guys."

As we walk behind the stage, I turn to Linus and muster saying: "Hey, I'm sorry about my mom and what she said to you last night... That was uncalled for. She's a bit nuts these days, ya know... Old people, I guess."

"Girl, I never met your ma."

"What? On Facetime... last night in the hallway."

"Nope, never met her. You okay, Stephanie?"

Baffled, I follow Linus closely as we wind our way around the back to the locker room. As we near our destination, it gets noisier and noisier.

"How many are there?" I ask Linus.

He doesn't answer, just holds the door open, nods at me and says: "Shall we?"

Let the madness begin!

"Hey, there she is!!" says a guy in a *Beavis and Butthead* shirt. He rushes over and starts to talk breathlessly into his microphone: "I'm Max at *W.X.M.C. Boston*, and I'm here with the AMAZING and COMPLETELY gorgeous Star Roberts!!"

I open my mouth to speak, but the journalist grabs back the mic.

"And there's the man of the moment! It's THE MOST FAMOUS RAPPER IN THE WORLD!" Max says into the microphone.

I look around and see THE MOST FAMOUS RAPPER IN THE WORLD saunter casually through the door, walk over to the radio presenter and put his arms around his shoulders as if he's greeting a relative. "Hey, man."

"So, dude, great to be talking to you on *W.X.M.C. Boston*. Tell me, how does it feel to be recording your new single with the gorgeous Star Roberts?"

This guy doesn't miss a beat.

"Oh, man, it's super-fly. She's the bomb," says THE MOST FAMOUS RAPPER IN THE WORLD, putting his arms around me. "We've got a great rap down and the new single will be out soon."

O.M.G., he actually hasn't met me yet! Still, I guess this is showbusiness.

"Want to tell our listeners on *W.X.M.C. Boston* what it's called?" says Max.

"Not yet, man," says THE MOST FAMOUS RAPPER IN THE WORLD. "It's still on the mixing board, but you'll be one of the first to know."

"It sounds great! Y'all got to go out there and download this shit when it comes out. I love Boston, man!"

I'm standing there with a rictus grin on my face, thinking: *Shiiiiiit, we haven't even recorded it yet!!! And did he just say "shit" on air?*

Max is now pointing the microphone at me: "And, Star, tell me more about the song because, although you've done great covers, I also know you're passionate about writing your own lyrics."

"Do you know what, Max?" I say. "I really am passionate about writing my own lyrics. And this song is really special to me, because I wrote it after a dream I had about my late husband and dad. It's about making your dreams happen and taking chances when you can, because life is really short, you know?"

"Yeah," says THE MOST FAMOUS RAPPER IN THE WORLD, "life is short, man. We on the clock, yo."

Like, seriously.

"That's great, guys!" says Max. "And now, if you wouldn't

mind, we'll just do some radio drops."

"Sure, man," says THE MOST FAMOUS RAPPER IN THE WORLD.

Max hands us a script, which we read aloud in parts and also together.

"Yo, I'm THE MOST THE MOST FAMOUS RAPPER IN THE WORLD," says THE MOST FAMOUS RAPPER IN THE WORLD…

"And I'm Star Roberts," I say…

Then we both say, together: "You're listening to *W.X.M.C. Boston*. NO OTHER PLACE FOR THE HITS OF TODAY!"

Except, I keep trying to speak over the MOST FAMOUS RAPPER IN THE WORLD's bit. And then we don't say the bit we're meant to say together at the same speed. It should be super-simple, but it takes a few times to get it right.

"Thanks, man," Max says, when he's finally happy with what he's got. "That was awesome, dude." He fist-bumps with THE MOST FAMOUS RAPPER IN THE WORLD, then does the same with me.

This routine is repeated around ten times, with ten different versions of Max, from ten different stations in the greater Boston area. It actually gets more fun the more we do, and by the end THE MOST FAMOUS RAPPER IN THE WORLD and I actually seem like we know each other… which is odd, seeing as it's only been fifteen minutes since I've even laid eyes on him.

"Hey, yo, thanks, man," says the MOST FAMOUS RAPPER IN THE WORLD, as we wrap up the tenth radio drop. "Li said you liked my hot sauce. That's dope. See you soon, girl."

And then he's gone again, whisked off by another woman. She takes him to a corner of the room where giggling fans – who probably paid an arm and a leg to get V.I.P. backstage passes – are waiting to take selfies with him.

Linus lumbers up to me. "Okay, you coming? We're going to the studio."

"Yes!" I say. "I am READY!"

I follow Linus through the corridors, and we walk past a massive lecture hall and a bunch of classrooms, a library and a canteen... I'm trying to take it all in, so I can tell Emily when I get home, and maybe even write it down one day...

And... Oy vey...! Bubby is ringing me again... What the...? It's the middle of the night in London, and I really can't take her call right now. I hit *"Decline"* and text her quickly:

"Recording, can't talk."

If it were life or death, or involved the kids, she'd have texted me in ALL CAPS. I'll have to get back to her. Oh, and Logan, too.

Eventually, we enter the smallest room I think I have ever seen – you know, it might actually be a cupboard. But I do not care. After forty-two years of hoping and praying, five years of working my ass off, months of planning, and three days of running around a weird town in Massachusetts, staying in the dumpiest of hotels, I am finally here! I am literally... In. The. Room.

"Right, I'll go and get him," says Linus. "Wait here."

I run my hand over the faders on the mini recording desk which has been set up, and pick up the microphone lying beside it, yet to be attached to its holder. I close my eyes and inhale deeply. This is it.

"Hey, man," says Z-Drive, coming in with a ton of cables. He pulls out the small table and starts to plug them into the mixing desk. "Enjoy the show?"

"OH, MY GOD!" I say. "It was incredible! He's so incredible. And then we did some interviews and radio drops. Incredible. Incredible. I can't wait to get recording. Is he coming? He is coming, right?"

"Yeah, man, he's coming, he's coming," says Z-Drive from underneath the table. "Chill."

Josh and the film crew have arrived at the closet-sized recording studio.

"Okay," I say, "we want as much of THE MOST FAMOUS RAPPER IN THE WORLD as we can, so why don't you go back and find Li, then follow him as he brings him here. Get the camera on him as much as possible!"

"Sure," says Josh, and they turn and walk back down the hall.

Z-Drive pops his head up from the table, attaches the

microphone to a stand and steps back, nodding slowly, pleased with the job he's done. Then he, too, disappears. And I'm alone again.

I sit on the corner of the desk for a few moments. Maybe it's minutes. Then I hear footsteps. A ton of footsteps, getting closer and closer. I put my head around the door of the recording studio/cupboard, and watch as THE MOST FAMOUS RAPPER IN THE WORLD and the entire posse head straight for me...

...And then straight past me.

The film crew is following behind, and Josh stops and looks at me, his eyebrows raised in question marks, as he points first at me then in the direction in which THE MOST FAMOUS RAPPER IN THE WORLD and his posse are quickly disappearing. He shrugs as if asking: "Should I stay with you or go after him?"

I mouth at him very slowly, feeling fury rise up within me: "HIM."

Chapter 12

"Double-Dealing Diva"

Do you know the best way to get back to your hotel from a college campus, at two a.m. on a January morning, when you're a singer who can't catch a world-famous rapper, and whose failing family-restaurant chain is about to be bought by the husband of her arch enemy on the P.T.A.? The Bitch of Belgravia? No? Then let me tell you: it's the school night bus no.235, which parks at pickup point B on the eastern campus roundabout. And this morning it contains me – full of sparkles and Dolce and Gabbana – and the driver, who is called Bill and kindly does not charge me.

As the bus winds its way through the dark city streets, past the police station where we registered Candice missing, the student health centre where we found out she was pregnant, and onward toward the mall, where I was first introduced to that incredible red sauce, I lean my head against the window and start to close my eyes. It's been a crazy few days. Pity none of it has been about what I came here to do.

My phone has been buzzing constantly since I picked up my bag and asked the security guard how the hell I was supposed to get back to my hotel, but so far I've avoided looking at the screen. Now it's buzzing again. Reluctantly, I take it out.

Fifty-seven missed calls from Bubby, and it's barely seven a.m. in the U.K. And a ton of messages. And a ton of notifications from my social media.

I press the Twitter icon, click on notifications and then @-*"mentions"*.

Oy vey! Barry has been tweeting again.

"@BarrySpeaks:

"Spotted with the Rapper! @StarRoberts is in Boston!"

There's a pic of me doing the radio drops. Man, how is he even getting a hold of this stuff in London?

I can't take much more of this. I flick back to the WhatsApps blowing up on my phone.

1x WhatsApp from Emily:

"Hey, Mom. Bubby is kinda upset. Can you call her back? X."

1x WhatsApp from Christina Wachman:

"Hey babe, I just wanted to say, Ben's offer, it's a friendly one. xox. C.W."

1x Logan:

"Mom! Our worries are over! I just sold half the nano-tracker biz to a bigshot V.C. firm in Tel Aviv!"

1x Alejandro:

"I know I'm obsessed. But, just a theory... maybe Mrs. Smart and Wachman are, like, having an AFFAIR?"

Oy fucking vey!

The night bus drops me a few blocks from the hotel. I climb down the steps and the heel of one of my boots snaps right off; I hobble back to the hotel. Damn, this is seriously depressing. I don't usually get depressed, and I typically make sure to see the positive and sunny side in everything I do. I have actually banned the kids from using super-negative "F"-words, like "fail", "fault" and "fear" but, I gotta say, hobbling back on my own in the cold and dark, in the wee, early hours of a freezing morning, to the Hotel du Slum, having quite literally watched a career-changing recording opportunity walk right past me... well, put as much positive spin as you like on it, Toto, but it all looks a teeny bit failure-ish to me.

The lights are on at the hotel, almost welcoming. I climb the icy steps and push open the squeaky door with half the gold stars scratched off. At least it's warm in here.

In the back of my mind is the thought that the student film crew did follow THE MOST FAMOUS RAPPER IN THE WORLD, so there is a tiny chance it could still happen tonight... although, what am I going to do at three a.m.? We're hardly going to record now, are we? Maybe my mother was right: maybe this is all a pipe dream. Maybe it's time to just accept this is just not going to happen, pack up and go home.

Still, there might be a chance. Maybe I'll just text Josh to see where he's at.

Ping!

What? That sounded a little too close to home. Maybe it was a coincidence.

I type another message:

"Hey, Josh, where are you, exactly?"

Ping!

That sounded even louder.

"Josh?" I say out loud, but as quietly as I can.

A head pops up from one of the comfy chairs in reception.

"O.M.G.! What happened to THE MOST FAMOUS RAPPER IN THE WORLD?"

"Hey, Steph. Yeah, so, about that…" Josh says, stifling a massive yawn.

I sigh heavily.

Josh looks pained. "C'mon, man, we're not the freakin' A-Team. The dude just totally disappeared into a car with his posse, and drove off really fast." He shakes his head. "I'm really, really sorry, Steph; we tried, but there was nothing we could do."

My phone is still buzzing in my handbag.

"It's okay," I say to Josh. "You should go to bed. I guess we just lost this one." I smile weakly. "Like, literally."

Back in my room, I kick off my broken boot and lie back onto the uncomfortable bed, relieved to be still for once.

My phone buzzes yet again. It's my mother.

I pick up warily.

"Mom?" I say. "You alright? It sounds kinda noisy where

you are."

"I just thought I'd better let you know, Stephanie," my mother says, importantly, "we are just outside Charing Cross police station."

"We?"

"Yes, Emily and I," says my mother.

"Why, Mom?"

"Well, in a moment," says my mother, "I will go into the station and give an official police statement, darling. If Emily would like to, she can come with me and experience the whole thing. I realize it's a school day, but I allowed her to take the day off, as I believe this is a situation which is particularly relevant to her education, especially if she's going to go to Harvard Law."

Harvard Law? Emily wants to be a lawyer?

What? Hang on, what? She took her out of school? What the...??

"What the hell is going on? You took Emily out of school?" I scream. "Are you kidding me?! Do you have ANY idea how ballistic the school goes about non-attendance these days!" Jeez!

"I did indeed take Emily out of school, Stephanie," my mother says, her voice curt. "And, I must say, send the school to me if they complain, because I absolutely stand by what I've done; it is of grave importance that she understands the severity of the current situation. This is about real-life criminality, the rule of law and the pursuit of justice! There is an entire school project on criminal justice right here!"

Hang on, what situation? What is my mother talking about? All kinds of crazy things are going through my head right now – none of them are particularly fun.

"Mom, okay, you're really not making much sense right now," I say. "Lemme talk to Emily."

"Hi, Mom," Emily says, a few seconds later. "We're at the police station! Did you get my voice message?"

"Yes, honey, I did," I say, feeling a little bit teary again. "Thank you, darling. I love you so much."

Emily says: "I love you, too, Mom; you're my hero. I can't wait to hear your new track with THE MOST FAMOUS RAPPER IN THE WORLD!"

"Sure, honey, I can't wait for you to hear it, either!" I say, as brightly as I can manage. "Er, so, what are you doing at a police station with Bubby?"

Silence.

"Emily," I ask again, "how is Beverly? I need to talk to her about the party."

Silence.

"Emily, are you hearing what I'm saying, honey? Is there something crackling on the line?" I take the phone away from my ear and tap on it, in a vain attempt to get a response.

Eventually, Emily speaks, her tone slow and deliberate: "Erm, I'm not exactly sure that I would say Beverly is great, Mom…"

"Emily, why would you say Beverly is not great?" I say slowly.

"Beverly is the greatest! You above all people LOVE Beverly."

There is another pause and I hear Emily sigh, heavily. Then she says, quietly: "Well, yes, I did love Beverly, but I'm pretty sure she's not feeling great right now, Mom." There is another big sigh, before my youngest child says: "Because, seriously, Mom, I mean... would YOU be feeling great if you'd just been locked up in jail?"

"You HAD MY NANNY ARRESTED? MOM?! What the actual fuck?!"

"Don't you swear at me, Stephanie Rachel!" my mother snaps, the phone passed back to her. "I did what was necessary."

My breathing has become slow and laboured. My nanny is in jail? What the hell is going on? My lovely, reliable, life-saving, kid-caring Beverly has been arrested? For what? What on Earth could she have possibly done? It would be an understatement to say that I wanted to puke.

"You know what's necessary, Mom?" Deep breath. "Having a professional, much-trusted nanny in the house, who is able to look after my children when I am six thousand miles away, on a career-defining work trip is freaking NECESSARY!"

"I told you not to swear at me, Stephanie," my mother says, shifting into iceberg mode.

I am now on the verge of shouting, as my face is going bright red.

"Mom, I need you to tell me, right now," I say, "why the hell is Beverly in a jail cell, when she's supposed to be doing the school run right now? You have to get her out of there!" I start to realize my sheer and utter dependence on this woman over the past few years. I hiss into the phone and cup the mouthpiece with my hand, so that anyone passing by doesn't hear.

"I'm certainly not getting her out of there," my mother says, firmly. "Beverly should be staying in a jail cell for a very long time. ESPECIALLY after what she's done to you."

"Mother," I hiss, "what EXACTLY has Beverly done?"

"Well," my mother sighs, triumphantly, "I did try and warn you earlier, when I followed her and watched her hand thousands of pounds over to an equally guilty associate…"

I am now curled in the chair, barely able to shake my head.

"Hi, Steph!" Candice walks past me, into the breakfast room. When she sees that I am on the phone, she stops and mouths: "Everything okay?"

I nod at her, in the same way that sometimes you just let your toddler eat the candy right before dinner, because at that moment you're tired and it's just easier.

Then I say: "Well, Mother, do tell… I'm all ears."

And so my mother tells me the story, which, if you were going to write it in a magazine, would be titled something like: *"How Beverly The Wonder Nanny Was Unmasked As Beverly The Criminal Mastermind, Because Bubby Bought A Pair Of £250 Pants."* Or something like that. Probably a bit shorter. You know, so it fits on the cover of *Vogue*.

Anyway, yes, a pair of £250 pants. Bubby had been shopping earlier in the week, and had bought a new pair of pants. They were a particularly expensive pair of black pants, as is the way of Chelsea. Then, in true Jewish-mother style, Bubby decided that, despite being absolutely gorgeous – beautifully lined, as well as comfy – she just couldn't justify them; there were plenty of better bargains to be had elsewhere. As she stood admiring herself, in the mirror in the guest bedroom, she decided the beautiful but over-expensive pants would have to be returned.

This should have been an easy process, except for the fact that Bubby had misplaced the receipt. She'd checked her purse and all her jacket pockets, but simply couldn't find it. In the end, she asked Gerald, who was convalescing and also didn't know where it was, but suggested that she might perhaps find it in the bag she'd taken the pants home in. Unfortunately, the bag was also nowhere to be found; Emily helpfully told her that it had probably already been tidied away in the basement, to a place known as the "Spare Bag Cupboard". As Emily told Bubby: "Mom always says you never know when you might need a spare shopping bag – especially if it's a nice one from Harrods." Gerald offered to go downstairs to the Spare Bag Cupboard, which is adjacent to Beverly's bedroom. And there, amongst a load of other Nice Spare Bags, he found The Bag from the King's Road boutique. In it, he found the receipt for the too-expensive pants, but also, curiously, a bunch of ripped-up bank statements. MY bank statements.

That night, Bubby, Gerald, Logan and Emily had sat down in the basement, Columbo-style, like a bunch of old detectives, painstakingly taping the bank statements back together. There were several occurrences over the past few months where cash withdrawals totalled several thousand pounds – way more than Beverly would normally need for food and stuff for the kids. There were payments made in Harrods and Selfridges which didn't make sense, either, for items which none of us had bought or requested. When they searched further, they found birthday and thank you cards I'd given Beverly, also ripped up, as well as cash-refund receipts from John Lewis, for gifts I'd given her.

Logan really loved Beverly, and was seriously bummed that this woman we all adored, loved and trusted so much could actually be a real-life thief and con artist, but he offered to help prove Bubby's theory, by planting his nano-tracker device into Beverly's bag, so that they could watch her movements. Sure enough, the incredible nano-tracker picked up a trip to the cashpoint around the corner from our house, then onto the pub where Bubby had photographed her handing over the cash to some guy.

I had to admit, it definitely looked like Beverly the Wonder Nanny was ripping us off. And, not only was she a fraud, she didn't seem to like us much, or the presents I'd given her, either.

So, Bubby had decided to confront Beverly. And, incredibly, although Beverly remained silent when Bubby told her she'd called the police, my nanny calmly got her bag and coat, made a cup of tea, and sat at the kitchen breakfast bar until the inspectors arrived.

I scroll through the pictures of the bank statements my mother has sent me. I can't bring myself to believe it. I am shocked, angry and in complete disbelief. But, even after finding this all out, I am furious with my mother for detonating this domestic disaster at the precise moment that I need my home to be calm and in control. Part of me feels like I should talk to Beverly, though I probably shouldn't... should I?

Maybe I just need to speak to the police.

"Mom, I am really unhappy..." I start to say. "I need your support here. I need Beverly. I am recording with THE MOST FAMOUS RAPPER IN THE WORLD. I need everything to be stable at home. I do not need the nanny in freaking jail!"

"Think about it, Stephie: do you want a criminal in your home or in jail?"

I do not want to hear any of this, let alone believe it. This woman was my saving grace; my friend! I feel truly and utterly betrayed.

"Do we know that she's a criminal for sure, Mom?" I ask. "I mean, couldn't you have waited 'til I at least got home? Or asked me to talk to her BEFORE you rang the police? I mean, c'mon,

Mom. I'm on the cusp of something life-changing out here; it's almost like you want me to fail."

My mother is silent for a moment.

"I do not want you to fail, Stephanie," she says, her voice crisp and determined. "But, trust me, your nanny IS a REAL criminal. And, from all the evidence, it looks as if she has stolen thousands of pounds from you. You, of all people, know your family is more important than anything. Having a known felon look after your kids and your home is a non-starter."

I can't think of anything else to say. She is one hundred per cent right and I feel one hundred per cent foolish, dependent and deflated. My mother, who suddenly feels like the voice of reason, speaks over my silence:

"I've got this, Steph. I am looking out for you and the kids. Now, go and finish up in the States, and get home soon. The investigating officer wants me to give a statement; I'll call you later."

I stare at the cracks in the ceiling, floods of tears streaming down my face. How could I have been so fooled? I trusted this woman with my KIDS' LIVES! I thought she loved us, but it was all just an act. Who the heck is this woman? Is she even really called Beverly? I'm enraged, completely betrayed. How could anyone take advantage of me like that? She was *family!* She played right into my distraction, with everything I have on my plate. Talk about taking my eye off the ball! It's mortifying.

I'm so sorry I left you, beautiful, says H.P.H., suddenly appearing and sitting on the edge of the bed, legs crossed. *But you got this! And there are so many people out there rooting for you and supporting you. Don't let this Beverly thing eat you up; learn from it. I told you a million times before, you are just so darn trusting! The kids are older now – move on. She ain't no Wonder Nanny after all.*

I turn as I hear a knock at the door. When I look back at the end of the bed, H.P.H. is gone again.

Knock. Knock. Knock. Again.

At this time? It's so late.

Knock. Knock. Knock. Knock. Knock.

"Okay, okay, for God's sake, I'm coming," I say under my breath, shifting my weight off the bed and walking, half asleep, over to the door.

Knock. Knock. Knock. Knock. Knock.

"Alright, alright. Jeez." I fumble with the night lock.

It's *him.*

He's wearing dark glasses, an American N.F.L. football shirt and absolutely STINKS of weed. And he's got the biggest smile on his face.

"Sorry about the knocking. Thought I might need to wake you up."

I look at my watch: 3:59 a.m.

"It's okay. I was awake."

"Well, then…" He waves the bottle of red sauce in my face.

"Come on, I'm hungry. We got important shit to talk about."

Chapter 13

ONE MONTH LATER…

LONDON.

"Success, honey, is all about persistence," H.P.H. would say whenever I was struggling. "If you persist, someday, trust me, you will get what you want."

I always used to reply that you could never take luck out of the situation, but H.P.H. didn't believe in luck. "It's about work, honey," he'd say. "The harder I work, the luckier I get."

I believed in luck, though. And so did Bubby, though she also believed in persistence, which she told me ran through our blood. My great-grandmother was the epitome of persistence: a woman who, after many aborted attempts, finally escaped the Jewish pogroms in Russia, by running across a cornfield with a stranger's abandoned baby strapped to her back. I was transfixed when my mom told me the story of her mother as a young teen, dodging the bullets flying past her, running both for her life and for a chance at a better life. The baby she was carrying got caught in some crossfire and died instantly.

That baby was HER guardian angel. Had she not carried that child, that bullet would have gone through her and I would not be here.

My grandmother Manya just kept on running, and didn't stop until she got to the docks. She escaped on a boat headed for New York. And, even when the boat had reached the Statue of Liberty in New York, the immigrant quota was up in the United States, so the boat made a sharp turn north, up to Canada. And there Manya made it to a new life. She persisted, she was lucky and she won. My mom tells me all the time that I remind her of her mother in a lot of ways.

I often wonder whether THE MOST FAMOUS RAPPER IN THE WORLD knocking on my hotel room door in the middle of the night and taking me for chicken wings – which he prepped and fried himself in the hotel's kitchen – was the result of luck or persistence. Maybe it was a bit of both. Anyway, they were astonishingly good wings. But the secret really was in the sauce...

It's a Tuesday night, a few weeks later, and I'm telling the story to Alejandro, who's sitting opposite me on the couch in the new green room, as Beaver does my make-up. I'm not sure either of us quite believe how it all worked out. How the rapper took me into the kitchen at four a.m., at the Hotel du Slum, made the wings and told me how Linus had come to him and told him about the problems at Café Michael, and how he'd had a lightbulb moment, realizing it was an opportunity for him, too. And how, as he egg-bathed, floured and spiced the wings, we talked about a deal which would eventually be hammered with the Wachmans, his sauce company AND The Pink Coconut, whereby the restaurant would get the investment it needed, the rapper would have a London eatery to launch his secret sauce... and The Pink Coconut would have a new venue, where together we could co-host our brand-new Café Michael Cabaret Nights, courtesy of the gang at The Pink Coconut.

And then the rapper did the most enormous *mea culpa* about not being in Boston and going M.I.A. The reason? An elderly aunt who lived in a residential home in Worcester, and who he'd promised his mother that he would see on a day trip from Boston. But – because we didn't have *enough* complications – the aunt got sick and his mother insisted he spend more time there. The location was going to have to change as the posse moved to Worcester, and they rearranged the tour dates so that he was able to spend as much time as possible with her.

Then his aunt's condition worsened and he wasn't happy with the medical care she was receiving, so he arranged for a top-level consultant to fly in from New York. On the night when we were meant to record, just after the concert, he'd just had a call from the home: his aunt was feverish and had asked to see her nephew. He went straight there, sat by her bed and held her hand all night.

"I just can't believe it," says Alejandro, as he sees Beaver rummaging through his mobile make-up vanity.

"Trust me, I couldn't, either," I say. "In the hotel kitchen, we literally talked for hours, bonding over chicken wings, discussing elderly relatives, juggling careers and kids. I mean, we actually laughed about having teenage kids! He even wanted to know what inspired me to write this song, and he listened intently to every word of the story, when I told him about H.P.H. and my dad coming to me in my dream."

"And what about the shooting? The whole palaver with the town being closed down suddenly?"

"So, I asked him exactly the same question…" I say, "…and he just said: 'What shooting, bro? Man, why do you think all we rappers do is shit with guns?'"

Ale smiles. "Well, he got you there."

"Yes, but he didn't get you *outta* there, did he, love?" Beaver smirks, brushing contouring powder all over my cheekbones and nose.

"No, he definitely did not," I say, and go back in my head to the rush on that last early morning in Worcester…

We had been booked on a flight back to London, leaving Boston at 8:55 a.m., so I knew it would be tight, but totally doable. With the troubles at home and Beverly in jail, I just wanted to get the heck home.

Except the inevitable happened: when we arrived at the airport, we learned that our flight had been cancelled – which, at the time, felt like the end of the world; I wanted to get home now! Back to my kids and my mom. Right now!

Fatigued and hungry, Candice, Beaver and I grabbed a coffee from a kiosk in the terminal, trying to figure out what to do next. The next flight which still had seats was the red-eye, leaving in ten hours! There was nothing we could do at that point. I was going to have to go outside and have an emergency cigarette.

Outside the terminal, I sat on my suitcase and looked around me. Business travellers were scurrying into departures with their carry-ons, briefcases and reusable coffee cups. Families were shepherding their children and a few studenty types with backpacks were faux arguing over whether or not to get doughnuts for breakfast. All this movement around me frustrated me even more. It felt like I was the only one not moving, not having a firm plan. Instead of plunging into problem-solver mode, I was sitting on my bag, no flight to take me home, smoking a bloody cigarette. And not sure who was going to help me this time.

"Steph, Steph!! You're being paged!! Come back inside!"

"What?" I turned around and struggled to hear what Beaver was saying, over the passing cars and shuttle buses.

"Steph! You're being paged to go to the V.I.P. waiting area."

"What does that mean? Where is that?"

"No clue, babe, but let's get a move on!"

As I went back into the terminal, Candice was already standing there with a Sky Cap, and all the bags on a large, portered trolley.

"What's happening, Cand?"

"I dunno, Steph. I was just about to pay for the red-eye and I heard them page you. The agent behind the ticket desk called someone from the V.I.P. area, and a minute later a Sky Cap shows up to get our bags."

The Sky Cap guy, in his mid-seventies, was certainly super-fit, as he hiked the cart with all our luggage toward the far end of the terminal and we continued to follow him down a ramp, through a long, long tunnel.

"We are walking under the runway, ma'am," he turned and said to me. "Always amazes me, that."

"Where are we going?" I said. "I'm a little bit freaked out, to be honest."

"The private aviation terminal, ma'am," beamed the Sky Cap, obviously proud that he gets to usher the V.I.P.s.

As we exited the tunnel, we headed into an elevator which took us up a few levels and opened directly into a beautiful glass foyer, overlooking a thin runway on the other side of the main international building. There was a not-so-small plane, with the tail number *"N2-S5G33"*, parked on the tarmac.

Candice turned to me and, as if in slow motion, said: "Holy shit, Steph…"

As we made our way onto the Global Express and sat on the plush sofa by the window, a nice-looking gentleman – late-forties, salt-and-pepper hair – approached me and said: "Morning, Ms. Roberts. I'm Captain John Flynn. It's an honour to have you on board today." Then he handed me an envelope. "Mr. Barry Lovett asked me to give you this."

"Who's Barry Lovett?" I said out loud. This was seriously like being on an episode of *Blind Date*, crossed with *Let's Make a Deal*, crossed with *The Ellen Show*.

"BARRY!!" screamed Beaver, immediately snatching the envelope out of my hand. "Well, this I gotta see!"

Beaver handed me back the envelope and opened the card. I held the envelope in my hands, running my fingers over the paper. *Shit, that must be at least 30 G.S.M.! That's heavyweight paper right there. That's not a crappy note.*

"What does it say?" I asked, slightly miffed.

"Dear Star," Beaver read aloud, *"please accept my deepest apologies for any hurt I have caused you. I ordered this especially for you, and hope it helps you get home in style.*

"Your greatest fan, Bx."

What the actual fuck? Nasty Tweeter Barry has sent me a private jet?!

When we got into our seats, a steward approached with a tray.

"Madam," she smiled, "welcome aboard. Glass of champagne?"

After we lifted off, I thought again about my "chickenfest" session in the kitchen...

THE MOST FAMOUS RAPPER IN THE WORLD knew *exactly* what his rap would be, as he popped on some earphones and played the M.P.3 of my track from his phone. Then, while leaning over the counter, he literally jotted down the lyrics to his rap on his cell phone, in his *"Notes"* app.

"Right, Star Roberts… we're good to go!" And, with that, he texted Linus and Z-Drive to get the studio ready in his "suite".

The suite – which was basically the same Hotel du Slum room I had, but with an extra living-room area and a small kitchenette – stunk of weed. In fact, there were plastic bags of the stuff literally scattered on the coffee table and the kitchen counter.

The sun had barely risen, and I had surely been up for at least thirty-six hours at this point, but I was running on more adrenaline than it takes to run a marathon!

I texted the young N.Y.U. film crew, who literally turned up at the door of the suite just seconds after I pressed *"Send message"*. Candice rocked up with Beaver, who magically made me look bright-eyed and bushy-tailed.

I sang, he rapped and we filmed it all. In fact, the N.Y.C. crew got exactly what they wanted: not just the amazing footage we wanted, but they also got high with THE MOST FAMOUS RAPPER IN THE WORLD. People often ask me if I did, too – but ladies never tell their secrets, do they?

"Wow, can you believe what we went through on that trip?" says Beaver, back in Café Michael, with a sigh. "To end up, just like that, on a private jet sent by BARRY, of all people? A private jet!

Insane," he reminisces.

"Insane. And how bizarre that THE MOST FAMOUS RAPPER IN THE WORLD wanted to invest in a London institution, to trial his hot sauce?!" says Alejandro.

"Insane, but bloody ingenious!" Beaver says, standing back to observe his work on my face.

"How do I look?"

"Fabulous. I'm just wondering what colour lippy..." Beaver says, picking up two lip-gloss tubes in almost identical shades of red, from his enormous make-up case.

"Oh, no... I think red makes me look old," I say.

"You always say that!" says Beaver, playfully slapping my arm. "I promise it won't make you look old."

"You always say that, too," I smile.

"Yeah, I do," says Beaver. "And it matches the jacket, too."

Beaver applies the stain, then brushes gloss over the top. "Lovely."

"Knock, knock." Christina Wachman tosses the words in my direction while standing under the doorframe to the room, air-knocking and smiling softly. "Mind if I come in?"

"I'll leave you guys in peace," Beaver says quietly, quickly blotting my lips and making a quick exit.

Christina hesitates a little, hanging by the door. "I just wanted to wish you good luck. It's a big night."

"Aw, thanks, Christina," I say, smiling warmly. "It is a huge night. You alright?"

"Getting there," Christina sighs. "There's been a lot of changes. Thankfully, it's all been mostly amicable, and I am feeling a wonderful sense of freedom."

Chelsea has been buzzing since the news broke that Christina and Benjamin Wachman have separated – and that Christina has moved in with Belinda Smart, the headteacher at Emily and Logan's school. Word is that their affair has been going on for YEARS. A true love match. No wonder Benjamin Wachman was always flirting with every other woman in town.

"Anyway, Ben and I really are so pleased that all this worked out," Christina goes on, waving her arms around the new green room at Café Michael, an old meeting area now full of mirrors, clothing racks, sofas and poster art from the European cabaret bars of the 1920s.

"Anyway, you'll do great out there; I know you will." She comes closer and hugs me; it feels genuine and warm. "Oh, Steph, K.C. would have been so proud of you."

"Hey, Steph!" Candice says.

Still able to conceal a very tiny baby bump, in a halter-style, floaty dress, Candice looks radiant as she stands at the door.

"Oh, wow, you look hot, hot, hot, girl!"

With a sweep of her hands, she asks: "Emily wants to come and give you a good-luck kiss. That okay?"

"Of course it is!" I say, sensing my daughter is nearer than

Candice is admitting, and I see her burst past my P.A. and run straight into my arms.

"Mom! Logan says he's already raised nearly twenty grand raffling tickets for his nano-trackers!" says Emily. "Isn't that incredible?!"

I embrace my daughter, smiling at my son's charitable spirit, which has since seen his place on the school football team reinstated. "It is, honey; it's brilliant. It's our time now."

"Are you ready?"

I look up to see Tony's head pop around the threshold. "Because they're all waiting for you, darling."

"Is he here?" I say, suddenly feeling a little nervous.

"Yeah, he's here. And the world's media are, too, by the looks of things. Jan's been doing a fantastic job as a bodyguard; certainly giving that guy Linus a run for his money. They're talking about letting Jan into the posse for the U.K. radio tour."

I smile. Lovely, lovely Jan, always there in a crisis. And, what do you know, he's also been doing some of the cooking since Beverly was arrested. He's actually pretty good, too.

I still can't believe Beverly is in jail awaiting trial. Turns out she has previous convictions for stealing and fraud under various aliases, so there is no way they're letting her out on bail.

"Good job, too," Bubby said, and I reluctantly agreed.

"So, are you ready, Star?"

Oh, she's ready, Tony. She's more than ready, H.P.H. says, appearing in front of me, the clearest I've ever seen him in this way; he's glowing, luminous and smiling. *Go get 'em, Dolly!* Looking directly at me, H.P.H. blows me a kiss then disappears. For the first time in a long time, I feel a sense of both peace for what has gone before and excitement for my next chapter.

"Yeah," I say, "yeah, I'm ready."

I hear the music start up outside in the main restaurant. So, I flick my hair over my shoulder, adjust my sparkly jacket and give myself the once-over in the mirror. Then I smile and take a deep breath. I can hear the warm-up act saying: "Ladies and gentlemen, please put your hands together for Star Roberts and THE MOST FAMOUS RAPPER IN THE WORLD!"

Tony hands me the microphone with a broad, warm smile. "I think you're absolutely ready."

"Yes, I truly am," I say, heading out onto stage. "But the real question, Tony, is: are they ready for me?"

THE END

How a Gangsta Rapper Made Me a Better Mom

Book Two

FOUR MONTHS LATER...

The narrow, cold corridor was bone-chillingly cold. And, my god, it smelled: the stench of people not allowed to take long baths; body odour so bad that it made me cover my nose and mouth with my hand. I reached into the pocket of my favourite Norma Kamali cargo pants and took out the lipstick-stained facemask I found earlier in my handbag. It was the only thing I was allowed to bring inside the prison. Everything else – my phone, my wallet, my passport, all my belongings – were left at the entrance, by the security scanner.

I stared at the tall, chunky guard as he pushed the door of a room open, and I noticed that his hand was completely covered in a colourful tattoo, from the tips of his fingers, continuing all the way up under the sleeve of his uniform.

Then I saw her: a very pale Beverly, sitting at a table wearing a prison-issue, washed-out, grey sweatshirt and matching pants.

She looked at me.

My reaction was to pull my mask down and fiercely stare right at her. I literally just stared. I couldn't speak. I had conjured all these things up in my mind about what I really wanted to say, but I seriously could not speak one word. I was just so hurt.

"Steph, I'm sorry. I'm really, really sorry," she said, breaking the silence. "I really needed the money."

"You lied to me, to my family," I blurted out. "I trusted you with EVERYTHING important in my life, and you completely betrayed me."

"I know…" She bowed her head and continued to speak, but I was not listening. I was thinking about my gorgeous kids, and that God knows what she may ultimately have done, had Bubby and Logan not caught her out.

The cockamamie excuses kept coming: "I was afraid"; "you were going through your own stuff"; "I was planning on paying it all back"; etc….

Oh, come on, Beverly. Blah, blah, blah, blah, blah…

I don't even know why I felt the need to go see her because, to be honest, whatever she said there and then, sitting in the emptiness of that room, I couldn't believe one word of it.

I realized afterwards that I needed to see for myself the con-artist and player that she was getting what she deserved. She was in prison because she got made. She had done this before and I was pretty sure she would do it again, if she didn't pay the price for it.

And now here I am… back in a bloody prison block.

I cannot believe it. This place is the pits. The walk to the holding cells is cold and grim. Once we got past the initial security checks – which were, let me tell you, pretty unpleasant – we were shown through a heavy, metal door and instructed to follow two neatly-dressed, monosyllabic guards, along a grey corridor lit with flickering strip-lights.

"So, I really think there has been a massive mistake here," I say to the guards. "An absolutely huge one, really."

Silence. These guys are saying nothing. Nada – or whatever "nada" is in Mandarin Chinese. They are as cold as freakin' ice. Or, about as cold as you'd expect Chinese state prison guards to be.

Candice looks terrified, and is protectively cradling her baby bump. No more pretending she's just eaten too much cake; my P.A. is most definitely "with child". She glances over to me, looking terrified, as I clasp her hand tightly to reassure her. At least she's happier now about the pregnancy, with everything about who the father is now out in the open. But I guess it's normal to feel terrified in her situation.

I mean, imagine if you'd just flown into Shanghai Pudong International, on what should be a super-exciting business trip, but instead of heading straight to the waiting limo outside, you had to redirect to an airport jail, because your boss's mother was holed up in there?

Oy vey! It doesn't matter where I go in the world, wherever there is trouble, Bubby is there.

As we traipse along the endless, dark corridor, I have some seriously eerie flashbacks to Beverly in the Charing Cross police station. The angry denials when I visited her left a bitter taste in my mouth, and my daughter Emily is still having nightmares about the whole mishegas. Our ex-nanny and part-time criminal mastermind is currently residing at Her Majesty's pleasure in H.M.P. Belmarsh, where she is awaiting trial for fraud and theft. I look around and think: *I really thought I was done with jails for a while.*

Candice whispers: "I really don't like it here, Steph. Do you think we're going to get her out? Also, do you think the baby can catch anything in here?"

The thing is, even if my mother is a total felon in the eyes of the Chinese state, I seriously owe her one.

"Stephanie, you're here! Get me out of here!" my mother wails theatrically, flinging herself against the cell bars. "I'm totally innocent! Whatever they say I've done... I... I haven't!!"

"Mom, calm down. I'm sure we can get you out of here."

I pause to check out her stark surroundings. "What have they said that you've done? From what I can gather, it's just about a visa you didn't apply for."

"But Gerald told me I didn't need one!"

"How would Gerald know that, Mom?"

"Oh, don't be silly, darling; he's a DOCTOR!"

Oy vey.

"Well, we need to get you the visa. Candice already called the Canadian embassy."

I look at the guards standing by the cell door, stony-faced.

"What has she done?" I say to them, adding under my breath: "I just wish I spoke better Mandarin, because you guys OBVIOUSLY don't speak English."

"Actually, I attended the London School of Economics," one of the guards informs me, in flawless, accentless received pronunciation. "And, before that, I was at a military boarding school in Kent."

Oops!

And, shit, no doubt they've got good hearing, too, since the place is probably bugged.

"Okay. What has my mother done?" I ask again.

"I'm afraid I can't tell you that, ma'am," says the guard who attended the military boarding school in Kent. "It's against protocol." He pauses, trying to suppress a grin. "As I said, your mother does not have the right visa," the guard continues. "In fact, she has no visa. She must procure said visa, otherwise she will remain in this detention centre and will be deported after twenty-four hours."

I turn to my mother: "Didn't you know this?"

"I'm pleading the Fifth, darling!" she says, leaning into the bars. Then whispers: "I think that's the safest thing until the ambassador arrives."

You'd think the visa would be an easy issue to solve: just fill in the paperwork, get the right form, fill in the right passport numbers, address, and declare you're not a criminal... Except the paperwork needed doesn't exist in the airport; the computer won't print one out. You're meant to do it in your home country, aren't you? So, the computer said no. Oy vey.

I'm pretty certain they don't have the Fifth Amendment here in China, and Bubby obviously does not realize that the only guy who's going to be turning up here is probably going to be a low-level wannabe flunky from the consulate. We ain't going to be seeing the Canadian ambassador in this shack. When I get my phone back, I'll see what I can finagle.

I look over and see that Candice is now biting her lip nervously. She might be over the initial hormone rush of the pregnancy, but she's still a wreck. I really don't want the crying to start now. For one thing, we don't have Beaver with us to fix any mascara mishaps.

"Well, I want a lawyer here, right now," I say, taking control of the situation, "and someone from the Canadian embassy. Right away!"

The guards, now returning to their native tongue, speak quickly between themselves, apparently discussing my request.

After a few moments, one guard nods at me and disappears through a side door.

"We will grant your request, Mrs. Bloom," says the remaining guard, "but it may take a few hours." He indicates that we should go back through the door, and I feel a sudden pang when I realize that my mother is not coming with us – at least, for the moment.

"I'll be back soon, Mom. I promise," I say, looking back at her. "We'll get you out of here!"

"Don't leave me, Stephanie!" my mother wails, theatrically. "I cannot be a victim of your fitness empire!"

Back outside the jail, the spring Shanghai sunshine is bright and cheerful. I look around for the car they promised to send me. My phone has been buzzing since I switched it on again, and predictably there are quite a few messages to catch up on.

WhatsApp from Barry:

"Star! Welcome to China! Let's conquer the sportswear world! B. x"

WhatsApp from Emily:

"Can't wait to see you in China, Mom… What did Bubby do now?"

What did Bubby do? Nothing to see here, ladies and gentlemen – other than the fact that we're trying to spring a pissed-off old lady from a Chinese jail. Oy vey, maybe trying to combine this business trip with the kids' summer break wasn't the best idea.

I update Alejandro on the Bubby situation.

"Jeez, Steph, what do you want me to say this time?" he says, harshly. "I mean, is all this worth it, just for a top that doesn't give you boob rash?"

TO BE CONTINUED...

About the Authors

Born and raised in Montreal, Canada, Stacey Jackson is a multi-award-winning singer/songwriter, T.V. presenter and entrepreneur. Having sung in bands since the age of fifteen, she also forged a career in T.V. and entertainment P.R. in New York for ten years, after graduating university. She now resides in London with her husband and four children.

Since putting her musical ambitions on hold to raise her family, Stacey re-entered the music world at the age of forty, when she recorded an album for the U.K. charity Music for Youth. The album, which raised £20,000 for the foundation, featured rock and Motown tracks she loved as a child and, although well received it, perhaps predictably, sunk without trace.

Except it hadn't.

The album was subsequently unearthed online by a D.J., who remixed one of the tracks and released it via the dance club scene. "Band of Gold" became an instant anthem, and catapulted Stacey to becoming a dance music icon. With her high-energy sound booming out across the nation's clubs and gyms, Stacey found herself performing on worldwide stages, from London to Las Vegas and Miami, and headlining at Pride festivals across the

U.K. and Europe.

She was approached by major record producers to co-write original dance and pop music, and has since been enjoying a successful career on the international music scene, with several chart-topping hits including her original song "Live It Up", featuring a collaboration with the notorious U.S. rapper Snoop Dogg. She also got to perform the song in a cameo appearance in Hollywood film *Reboot Camp*, ten years later.

In 2021 Stacey became the presenter of the nostalgic music series *Stacey Jackson in the 80s*, where she wrote, produced and shot 54 episodes for three consecutive seasons of the series for the Sky Music channel *Music and Memories* (formerly known as *Spotlight T.V.*). The series theme song "Flipside", written by Stacey, garnered the number one spot on the Global Digital Radio Charts in 2022.

Stacey is also the founder and chief designer of technical fitness brand, Staefit, which includes a patented sports top she created, to help large-busted women find the support they need while working out, without having to wrestle to get in and out of their fitness clothes. She is a voting member of the Recording Academy, a patron of the Serpentine Arts Council and a supporter of numerous charities in the arts and medical fields.

Stacey continues to spread her message, "It's never too late to live your dreams," and, fittingly, is one of the celebrity judges on the esteemed panel for Talent is Timeless, the global talent competition aiming to discover extraordinary musical artists over the age of fifty.

For additional information about Stacey Jackson, scan here:

Ruth Elkins is a British writer, journalist and editor, most recently at *The Times* of London and at *MailOnline*. With over twenty years' experience writing and editing for some of the world's leading publications, including *The Guardian* and *Sky News*, she has written on everything from Eurovision to "Environmental Porn", and was once dubbed "The Babe of Berlin", after she wrote in a column that German men couldn't flirt.

She spent six years living and working in Berlin, is a Faber Academy "Writing a Novel" graduate, and her short fiction has been published alongside Alain de Botton's. As well as her own fiction writing, she helps others find their own stories and hone them into great, captivating narratives.

Acknowledgements

I could not have done this without my incredible writing partner Ruth Elkins, who has been by my side since the beginning of my professional musical journey. Her talent and wit helped to create and develop these strong, fictional personalities, and added extra sparkle to the pages. Thank you for coming on this adventure with me.

To the amazing veteran author Nancy Lamb, your valuable experience gave us the push we needed.

A huge thank you to Colin Starr, Adam Langston and Ramzi Sleiman for joining this ride, and helping me to give all the characters their own voices and melodies.

To my real "besties" dotted around the world (you know who you are), who have been rooting for me from the start, I love you all madly! Your friendships mean the world to me. And, of course, Lea Salomone and all of Team Stae – past and present – who have been helping me to climb that music-biz mountain, and everything that comes with it.

A huge shout-out of gratitude to Steven Machat, who not only introduced me to "The Most Famous Rapper in the World", but inspired me to tell the tale. As well as to all at L.R. Price, who believed in me and our ability to tell a story.

And, last but not least, a ginormous thank you to my husband, Henry, my rock and my biggest cheerleader, who has put up with me for decades – particularly as a night owl (I promise I won't turn the lights on anymore in the middle of the night)! Henry, your feedback and guidance along the way was not only paramount to this project, it kept me grounded. I couldn't imagine my life without you. I love you forever and always.

To all of you, I am sincerely indebted.

A Little Yiddish History

Growing up, my family and I adhered to some of the Jewish traditions passed down from generation to generation, but we were not particularly religious at all. Although I did go to a Jewish school where I learned to speak Yiddish and Hebrew (as well as French, as I grew up in Montreal), we did not eat kosher, my dad and brother never wore a kippah (Jewish word for skullcap) and we almost never went to a synagogue. Even though I spoke the language reserved for Jews of Eastern European descent (which was also written phonetically in Hebrew letters), I thought of myself as Jew-*ish*. Speaking Yiddish, however, helped me communicate with my own "Bubby" (the Yiddish word for "grandmother"), whose primary language was Yiddish, and her English was really not that great.

Yiddish is a very special (and, unfortunately, almost obsolete) language. Some of the Yiddish literature, poems and plays I studied in school were written in the late 1800s/early 1900s by the likes of Shalom Aleichem, Isaac Bashevis Singer and I.L. Peretz. These stories not only made me appreciate the uniqueness and nuances of the language but, more so, helped me connect to my own heritage, either by understanding the plight of the author's storytelling (during the wars, for example) or appreciating the ability to find humour in unbearable situations, as with the comedic writings of Shalom Aleichem. The combination of studying the language, speaking with my bubby and belonging to a tight knit small Jewish community in Montreal was integral to formulating my identity growing up, and how I still use some of the fabulous Yiddish words and expressions, even today.

After graduating with a communications degree from university, I moved from Montreal to New York. It was certainly easy to retain my "Jewishness" there; in Manhattan they even suspend alternate side-parking on the Jewish New Year! New Yorkers – no matter what race or religion – had a certain knowledge, respect and admiration for the Jewish culture, and when it came to Yiddish, it was common to use some Yiddish words in English phrases – especially when there wasn't a good English word or phrase to really describe what they were trying to say. As a result, some of the popular Yiddish words (such as *"schlep"*, *"glitch"* and *"schpeil"*) have made it into the English dictionary, and are also sprinkled throughout *How a Gangsta Rapper Made Me a Better Mom.*

Glossary of some Yiddish words frequently used in the book:

Alta Kakker: Literally means *"old fart"*: *"Bubby's boyfriend, Gerald the octogenarian, was spritely for an alta kakker."*

Bar Mitzvah: The religious initiation ceremony of a Jewish boy who has reached the age of thirteen, and is regarded as ready to observe religious precepts, and eligible to take part in public worship. A Jewish girl would have a "Bat Mitzvah".

Bashert: Destined or intended. Stephanie meeting her future husband at a club in Florida was *"bashert"*.

Bubby: Jewish/Yiddish term for "Grandma".

Dreidels: Spinning tops played during the holiday of Hanukkah.

Farklempt: Choked up or speechless.

Farmished: Confused or mixed up.

Haimish: Homey: *"Our house is very haimish."*

Hanukkah: Also known as the "Festival of Lights"; a Jewish holiday commemorating the recovery of Jerusalem and subsequent rededication of the Second Temple, at the beginning of the Maccabean revolt against the Seleucid Empire, in the 2nd century B.C.E. The festival usually falls around Christmas time, and those who celebrate both holidays have used the term *"Chrismakka"*.

Kosher: Refers to a Jewish dietary framework for food preparation, processing and consumption, which orthodox or very religious Jews follow. Food which orthodox Jews do not eat (such as pork or shellfish) is called *"traif"*. In English, when you hear something that seems suspicious or shady, you might say: "That doesn't sound kosher." In the book, Bubby is suspicious of Wanda *"doing something not kosher"*.

Kvetch: To whinge or whine.

Matzah balls: Matzah balls or matzo balls are Ashkenazi Jewish soup dumplings, made from a mixture of matzah meal, beaten eggs, water and a fat, such as oil. Matzah balls are traditionally served in chicken soup and are a staple food on the Jewish holiday of Passover.

Mazal tov: A Jewish phrase expressing congratulations. The phrase is also often used to wish someone good luck.

Mishigana: Someone who behaves a little bit crazy or absurd.

Mishegas: Crazy or senseless activity or behaviour. Craziness.

Nosh: To nibble or have a light snack. In the book, Steph isn't a big "nosher"; she likes to watch her weight.

Oy vey: Phrase used especially to express exasperation or dismay: *"Oh, woe!" "Oy Vey is meir,"* means: *"Oh, woe is me."*

Putz: A fool; an idiot.

Schlep: To haul or carry (something heavy or awkward): *"She schlepped her groceries home."* Also referring to something as a long trek: *"It's such a schlep to drive all the way out to the country."*

Schmearing: To spread (like *"schmearing"* butter on bread). In the book, Beaver is *"schmearing bronzer on Stephanie like Nutella on a bagel."*

Schpatzing: Strolling. Stephanie likes to go *"schpatzing up and down Chelsea's fashionable Sloane Street."*

Schtick: A gimmick, comic routine, style of performance, etc., associated with a particular person: *"There are many great comics who have based their stand-up shtick on observational comedy."*

Schvitzing: Sweating: Stephanie *schvitzes* from anxiety after she swallows her iPad stylus cap.

Shikse: A non-Jewish woman, all too often used derogatorily. It can also have the connotation of "young, blonde and beautiful." Referring to a man's gentile wife or girlfriend as a *"shiksa"* implies that his primary attraction was to her good looks.

Shpeil: A lengthy or extravagant speech or argument usually intended to persuade. However, this word also means to "play" (as in a game) in Yiddish.

Shtetl: Small Jewish town or village from eastern Europe. Even though Steph was from Canada, she lived in a primarily Jewish neighbourhood, which felt like living in a *schtetl*.

Tuchas: Slang for rear end, bum or butt.

Yenta: Female busybody or gossip. In the book, the P.T.A. moms all like to gossip; they are all *yentas*.

About the Publisher

L.R. Price Publications is dedicated to publishing books by new authors.

If you are an author interested in getting your book published, or a retailer interested in selling our books, please contact us.

L.R. Price Publications Ltd,
27 Old Gloucester Street,
London, WC1N 3AX.

For additional information about Stacey Jackson, scan here:

Printed in Great Britain
by Amazon